Black Magic Kitten

by

Sara Bourgeois

Blurb

Welcome to Coventry!

Kinsley Skeenbauer never thought she would go home. At seventeen, she'd left Coventry and didn't look back. But after a messy divorce, she packed up her stuff and drove toward the only place that she knew would accept her.

Life hadn't been easy for Kinsley since she left town. Despite wanting a family desperately, she was childless. She had a college degree but had just been fired… again…

She'd spent her entire adult life rebelling against what she was, and that meant hiding her true self from the world. Kinsley left Coventry on a mission to be ordinary.

But you know what they say about the best-laid plans…

Coventry isn't your typical small town. It's home to the most powerful family of witches in the world. Two ancient witch families united when her parents married, and she was supposed to be their leader.

Nobody ever asked Kinsley if that's what she wanted, though. Funny how the universe worked because there she was divorced, childless, and jobless… again… rolling into Coventry in her broken-down car with a U-Haul full of everything she owned.

The joyous welcome home party was short-lived, because a dead guy turned up, of all places, behind the diner.

Of course, the town's hunky sheriff starts to give Kinsley the side-eye. But a lot of people wanted the victim dead, and that only complicates the investigation.

There's a murderer on the loose in Coventry, and Kinsley's got to learn to harness her powers to avoid the killer's snare.

Oh! And, then there's Meri, the black cat familiar. Someone decides to grant him one wish for his faithful service to his coven, and it doesn't go as planned either...

Welcome back to Coventry. The events in this story take place thirteen years after the final scene the Wicked Witches of Coventry series. It can be fully enjoyed on its own and is suitable for all ages. You'll find no swearing, gore, or adult situations, but you will find magic, mystery, and a hint of lighthearted mayhem.

Chapter One

"No! No! No!" I yelled to no one in particular and hit the steering wheel hard enough to hurt my hand.

Then I realized there was a car coming from the other direction, and I had to pull over as safely as possible before I caused a horrible accident. My car's engine lasted long enough for me to guide it and the trailer I was dragging off to the shoulder, and then it died completely.

I was a couple of miles out from Coventry. I'd almost made it home.

My cell phone showed no signal. You'd have thought with all the new technology, they could get a signal out there. I was sure even Coventry had to have one of those newfangled towers, but alas, the phone was useless.

No matter what the scientists came up with, the ley line in Coventry could destroy it. Earth's magnetic something or other, according to them, but I knew it was magic.

I had two choices. I could wait there on the side of the road for someone to come along and rescue me, or I could do something I hadn't done for at least thirteen years.

Inside of me somewhere was the power to make that engine behave and get me the rest of the way home. All I had to do was wave my hand over the errant engine and focus my intention. I was out of practice, but I still knew how it was done. By the time I'd quit my magical studies to go to regular school, I was more accomplished than most adult witches.

No one had really pressed the matter when I refused to take magic seriously again after they pulled me back out of regular school either. I dithered around doing the bare minimum until I ran away at seventeen, but I still understood enough to get me in big trouble.

But I wasn't ready yet. At some point, I'd have to go back to being a witch. It would be the price for returning to Coventry.

I was not giving in yet.

After I popped the hood of the car, I went around and slid my hand under to find the latch. When I had it opened and propped up, I tied the flag from the safety kit I kept in the trunk to my side-view mirror and got back in.

A couple of cars did go by, but they were both self-driving. It figured. Even out in the sticks, I was the only one left driving a twenty-year-old Subaru. Oh, well, I loved her. I'd paid for that car with my own money after the divorce with Gavin had left me high and dry.

I found out that's what happens when you marry a lawyer who is friends with no one but other lawyers.

I couldn't even find someone decent to represent me, but by the end, I didn't care.

You see, I'd caught him cheating on me, and somehow, he and his shark lawyer friends ended up making me look like the bad guy.

I'd been indignant and full of fight in the beginning, but a year and a half into the proceedings and the weight of catching the love of my life with my best friend and then having him smear my name in front of everyone we knew had taken its toll. I'd stopped fighting and let him ruin me so that I could just walk away from the mess.

The icing on the cake had been that one of his best friends was also good friends with the woman who owned the company I worked for at the time. I'd received my walking papers the week before. He'd gotten me fired one week after taking everything in the divorce.

What I did have was an envelope full of cash stashed in the back of my closet. Somehow, I'd known to save for a rainy day. I hadn't been able to add anything to it since Gavin and I had separated, but I'd squirreled away what I could while we were still together.

It wasn't much when you considered how wealthy we'd been, but at least it was something. I'd thought there was only $2,000 in it, but when I checked it as I was packing, there was $7,000.

I took a cab over to the nearest discount car dealership, because I'd had to turn my Mercedes over when the divorce was final, and I'd bought the Subaru with half the money. What I had left was enough to rent the U-haul, buy out the last couple months of my apartment lease, and eat value menu hamburgers until I got to Coventry.

The car hadn't been as great of a deal as I'd thought, though, because there I was sitting on the side of the road waiting for someone to come by and rescue me.

By the time it started to get dark and I'd eaten the rest of my snacks, it became evident that no one was going to rescue me. I took out my phone again and hoped that maybe at night I could get a signal. I didn't, but that didn't stop me from getting out of my car and standing in the middle of the road trying. I reached my arm up into the air to see if it helped to get the phone higher. It didn't, and how would that have helped anyway? It's not like I could talk to anyone with my phone up in the air like that. Maybe they could have heard me on speaker, I reasoned.

No matter. There was no signal. I was in one of America's last dead zones. I sighed and put the phone in my pocket.

I also needed to get out of the middle of the road before one of those self-driving cars ran me over. I still didn't trust those things.

The way I saw it, I had two choices. Well, three if you counted sitting in my car all night waiting for someone who wasn't coming to come along.

My other two choices were to use magic to fix the car or start walking. It took me a while to decide. I wanted to just walk. It was only two miles, but then I remembered that it was two miles along a deserted highway in the pitch-black dark.

I'd heard enough stories about the woods around Coventry to know it wasn't a good idea to be out there at night. My parents and family would talk about things when I was supposed to be asleep.

I wasn't asleep, though. I was usually sitting at the top of the stairs listening. Meri would be there too, but he'd never tell on me. I bribed him with bacon, so he'd happily keep me company while I eavesdropped.

Sometimes they would talk about the time Mom and Dad discovered zombies in those woods. The very ones I could see from the road where I was standing.

The witches in our family were powerful enough to raise the dead. Some of them were powerful enough to raise the dead but also clumsy enough to unleash all manner of demons and horrible ghosts on the world. I don't know that any of them ever learned their lesson either. They would just clean up their messes and live to cast another day.

Then there was also Uncle Brody. He died when I was a baby, but his spirit never crossed over. Mom didn't know it. Sometimes when I was a kid, I would see him outside my window. Even then, I could almost feel him out in the dark watching me from behind a tree.

As I lived in the real world and my magic faded, it was harder and harder for him to reach me. It got to the point where he could only visit me in nightmares. I'd stopped having to worry about being out too late and having his angry specter following me home. I could even forget to close the curtains before dark without finding him there looking in at me.

But just then, with the moon out and shadows falling from every tree, I could sense that he was close again. Something told me that he had to get to me before I got to Coventry. Once I was back home, the ley line would make me invincible to his malice.

That made up my mind for me. I quickly ran my hands above the engine. "Please start. Come on, baby. I promise I'll take good care of you if you'll just get me out of here."

I didn't know any spells for fixing cars. What I did know was how to focus my intentions. As long as the car started, that was all I needed.

After I slammed the hood down, I rushed around to the driver's side and got in. I knew not to look in the direction of the trees to my right. My brain was screaming at me not to look, but I did.

He was there. Brody stood at the tree line staring at me. It was the first time he had manifested himself into the world, at least in my presence, since around the time I got out of college.

I turned the key and prayed to the Goddess I'd abandoned that it would start. "Come on, please. I will do what I was put on this Earth to do if you just get me home safe."

It was a promise I knew I'd never be able to take back, and one that I was happy I made when I saw Brody's ghost running towards my car.

The engine roared to life, and I didn't hesitate to put the pedal to the floor. It was just a Subaru and not a stock car, but she was fast enough. Except that I forgot I was towing a trailer and nearly jack-knifed off the road.

"Stay on!" I yelled as the car swerved. "Drive straight. I'm going home!"

Whether it was magic or just good driving skills, I was able to get the car going straight without running off the side of the road or breaking the trailer hitch. I looked back using the rear-view mirror and saw Uncle Brody's ghost standing in the middle of the road. He looked furious, but he knew he couldn't follow where I was going. I would be safe from him once I reached Coventry.

And at the speed I was going, I'd reach it sooner rather than later. I slowed down a little as the town sign came into view.

It wasn't too late. I could still go back.

"To what?" I asked myself with a slightly hysterical laugh. I had nothing to go back to.

Everything in my life was gone. Except Coventry.

I rolled into town and even though it was dark, there were still people out milling around. Most of them turned and stared at me like I had at least three heads. Some were probably because they recognized me while the others saw nothing but a stranger driving into their town in a beat-up old car after dark.

When I passed the bed and breakfast, I briefly considered pulling in. I could stay there for the night and not bother my parents until the next morning. They didn't even know I was coming. I hadn't called.

They would know soon enough, though. I'd already seen a couple of the Aunties, and they'd be on the phone with my parents in a heartbeat.

I drove the rest of the way to my parents' street but I sat down the road for a while. It was like I was begging the Universe to give me one more shot at not coming crawling back home.

It was not meant to be. Nothing happened except I wasted more time. Plus, I'd just made the promise to embrace who I was.

"Being a witch isn't bad, Kinsley," I said to myself. "You're just being a spoiled brat. You're mad because you were wrong, and you don't want to admit it. You never should have left and now you feel like a fool for having to come crawling back."

But I knew my parents would take me back with open arms. Even if I hadn't visited them in thirteen years. Tears began to spill down my cheeks. How prideful and stubborn I had been.

It didn't matter if I had to move back in with my parents at thirty. As I pulled into the driveway, my heart began to pound.

All of the lights were out at Hangman's House. The place looked completely abandoned. I hadn't seen my parents, but I had spoken to them. Neither of them had mentioned going on vacation or moving away.

Maybe they are just in the back of the house, I thought.

I walked up the front steps and considered whether I should just walk in or knock first. It was the house I had grown up in, but Hangman's House hadn't been my home for a long time.

When I raised my fist to knock, the door popped open. "Okay," I said. "Hello?"

No one answered, but the door opened a little more. Having been raised in Coventry, my first suspicion was ghosts.

It was also possible that the house itself just wanted me to come in. Hangman's House had a mind of its own, and it tended to do little things to manipulate its inhabitants' lives.

"Hello?" I said again as I stepped through the door. "Is anyone here? Mom? Dad?"

I looked around and the furniture was all gone. There was also no… stuff of life… There was no furniture, but there was nothing else to indicate that people lived in the house either. There were no books, magical supplies, trinkets, or photos on the walls. The house looked completely abandoned.

"What in the world?" I asked as I took a step deeper into the living room.

It was right then that red and blue lights flashed across the walls. The blip of a siren followed.

I froze. My parents weren't in the house, and I had no proof I was even supposed to be there. My stomach clenched at the thought of spending the night in the Coventry jail. People would be talking about it for months. I'd be the butt of every joke for at least a few weeks.

Unless they were still too afraid of me. "What is wrong with you?" I asked myself. Going to jail was worse than being made fun of. I had my priorities all out of whack.

"Come out with your hands up," a male voice announced over the cruiser's speaker.

"Okay," I called out. "I'm coming out."

I walked out slowly with my hands raised up. The sheriff had his hand over his gun, but he relaxed when he saw me. I guess I either wasn't that threatening or I wasn't what he'd expected.

Or both.

"I'm sorry," I said. "I swear I didn't break into the house. This is… was my parents' house."

"You can put your hands down and walk down here. Do it slowly, though, and keep your hands where I can see them."

The front step creaked loudly under my foot. The old wooden treads needed to be replaced badly. It seemed off to me. My parents never would have neglected the house. There was only one thing that it could mean, and that was Hangman's House was not happy about my return.

"You say you're Brighton and Remy's daughter?" the sheriff asked me. "That makes you Kinsley Skeenbauer, correct?"

"Yes." I shook my head along with my answer.

"If that were true, you'd know they don't live in the house anymore," he said skeptically.

"You would think so," was my only answer. "Are you going to arrest me then?"

"Let's not get ahead of ourselves. It's not that late. I'll give your mother a call. She and your father are over on Hallows Road."

"His old house," I said.

"Well, if you know that, you might actually be their daughter," he said. "Give me a minute."

He took out his phone and punched in a number. His intense blue eyes wandered up from the ground and met mine. A brief smile pulled at the corners of his mouth before he caught himself and went back to his stern "law enforcement face".

"Hey, Brighton, this is Thorn... I'm good. How are you?"

Thorn. Where did I know that name? I wondered. It sounded really familiar.

"I'm glad to hear it," Thorn said. "I'm doing pretty well myself, but hey, I've got a question for you. I'm sorry to disrupt your evening, but I've had an incident at Hangman's House. No, I'm fine and the house is fine, but I caught a woman inside. She says she's your daughter, but I have to confirm that." He looked at me again. "Around five-five with long auburn hair and green eyes. A few freckles across the bridge of her nose." He was describing the way I looked, and I couldn't help but blush a little when he described my freckles. I had no idea what was wrong with me, but it made my stomach do a little flip-flop. "Okay, Brighton. I'll take a picture really quick. Hang on." He aimed the camera at me and took my picture. "I sent it. Okay. Yes. Thank you so much, Brighton. Have a good night." He hung up.

"So, am I under arrest?" I asked when he put his phone away.

"She said it's you."

"I know that," I said with a chuckle. "Sorry to cause problems, officer."

"You can call me Thorn," he said.

"I don't mean to pry, but that name sounds familiar. Maybe my mother had a friend named Thorn a long time ago? But you look too young to be one of my mother's old friends," I said.

"You're talking about my father," Thorn said. "He was friends with your mother and sheriff of this town until my mother made him move away. I'm actually Thorn Junior."

"Well, it's nice to meet you, Thorn Jr. Sorry it was such a rocky start," I said.

Thorn's sapphire eyes sparkled a little when he laughed and said, "I'm actually glad you're not a burglar, Kinsley. Not having to arrest you and do the paperwork will make my night much easier."

Just then his radio came to life. Dispatch called him about some teenagers out in a field. The farmer was worried they were going to tip his cows and said the law better get out there fast or he was going out with his shotgun.

"Tell him to hold his horses, Betty. I'll be right there," Thorn responded. "I've got to go. I guess I'll see you around?"

"You will," I confirmed.

"A pleasure to meet you, Kinsley."

"Hey, one thing really quick. Did my mom say she was coming this way?"

"As soon as she and your father get dressed," Thorn said as he ducked back into his cruiser. "Good night."

"Good night," I said with a wave.

Once he'd pulled out of the driveway, I could see something on the other side of his car. It looked like a shadow barreling toward me across the field next to the house.

I squinted my eyes to see what was coming toward me. It took a second for me to figure it out because I only had the light of the moon to help me see. It wasn't a shadow.

It was a cat.

Chapter Two

Meri ran up to me and leapt into my arms. He rubbed his head against my chest and began to purr so loudly that it vibrated right to my heart.

I just stood there for at least five, maybe ten, minutes holding him. Tears ran down my face, and I couldn't believe how much I'd missed him. I hadn't known he could even purr that loud.

After a while, I finally said, "We should go inside." I set him down and started walking toward the house.

"You're not going to tell anyone about that?" he asked. "Right?"

"About what?" I asked and smiled at him over my shoulder.

"Whatever… creature," he said and sashayed past me through the front door.

"Now, there's the Meri I know," I said with a laugh. "It's good to see you again. I missed you so much."

"Well, if you hadn't abandoned your home and family, you wouldn't have that problem now, would you?" he shot back at me.

"Ouch," I said.

"Just being realistic," Meri said. "It is good to be back in this house, though. The other one is so boring."

"Why did they move? Why wouldn't they stay here at Hangman's House?" I asked.

"The house has been cursed since you left. They finally got tired of dealing with it a couple of years ago and moved into Remy's old house. Thank gawd he didn't sell it," Meri said with a flick of his tail. "But, now you're back and you can make it right."

"With the house?"

"Yeah. Please tell me you haven't forgotten everything, Kinsley. That head of yours should have been hollow enough to stuff a few memories into."

"Wow, you are exactly how I remember you," I said.

"You wouldn't have it any other way," Meri retorted.

"Whatever."

"Whatever."

"So, my parents are coming?"

"What do you think?" Meri asked.

"Are they mad?"

"Kinsley, come on."

"At least it's too late for them to throw a huge party tonight," I said.

"You think so?" Meri asked. "Anyway, let's go inside. Maybe if you promise to stay, the house will let you turn the lights on."

I picked up Meri and started for the front door.

"I can walk, you know," he said.

I gave him a squeeze and a kiss on the head.

"Yuck." But he started to purr again.

Back inside the house, I tried the light switch next to the front door. Nothing happened.

"I'm sorry," I said. "I will stay. I'm here to stay."

I tried the switch again, and the lights came on. They were quite dim, though.

"I promise. Coventry is my home, and I intend to stay."

With that, the lights brightened to normal levels. I looked around the living room of the house I grew up in and sighed.

The lack of furniture would be an issue. I didn't have much of that in my trailer.

"Looks like I'll be sitting on the floor," I said.

"Meh, not really. The attic in the library still has all its furniture. Your parents left that intact. You just have to hang out up there. Having guests over might be a problem," Meri said.

"I wasn't planning on having many guests," I said. "I hoped I could just keep my head down and maybe get a job. I don't want a lot of attention."

"You're hilarious," Meri said.

"What do you mean?" I asked.

"Come on, Kinsley. If you don't think your family is going to make a huge deal out of you coming home, then you clearly took a bump to the head."

"But I ran away. They should all be mad at me. It should take time for them to warm back up to me. Years even," I said.

"Ha ha. I think you really did hit your head. You don't remember your own family? Do you think they're going to punish you for living your life the way you wanted? For doing things on your own terms?" Meri asked.

"But I broke my father's heart when I left, didn't I? And I never visited. I was afraid if I came back, even for a visit, I'd never get away again," I said.

"How'd that work out for you?"

"What are we talking here? Break it down for me," I said.

"I imagine there's going to be a party here. In the back. The whole coven, and probably the whole town, will be invited. You'll be the center of attention for hours on end."

"Ugh," I said.

"Hey, you could have listened to me thirteen years ago and just stayed," Meri said.

"No, I couldn't have. I would have always wondered. My life here would have never felt settled," I said.

"And it will now?" Meri asked.

I shrugged. "Yeah. I learned my lesson. I had to do it the hard way, but it's learned."

A knock at the door ended our conversation.

"I wonder who that could be," Meri said.

"I don't know. Who knows I'm here?"

"The sheriff and your parents," Meri said. "Unless your mother already started calling people. That's entirely possible."

"I'll just get it." I looked out the peephole, and it was my parents. "What are you doing knocking?" I said as I opened the door. "This is your house."

My mother pulled me into her arms. I felt my father wrap his arms around both of us. Last was Meri who rubbed against my legs and then sat on my feet.

For a while, we all just stood there. At some point, I started to cry. My mother just stroked my hair and kissed my cheek.

Eventually, we broke our embrace. My mom was smiling, but tears were running down my dad's cheeks. He pulled me back into a hug and mom stood back as he held me for a while longer. "My little girl," he said and kissed the top of my head.

His hair had gone nearly gray, but it started to change to a deep chestnut right before my eyes. My mother went from gray to fire engine red curls.

"Your hair," I said.

"What is it?" Dad asked.

"Both of you. Your hair is turning red," I said. "Bright red."

"Wow, that hasn't happened for a long time. It must be because you're here with us, darling," she said. "And yours..."

"What? What's going on with mine?"

I ran into the bathroom to look. I could remember my mother's hair changing to funky colors when I was little. It happened every time she unlocked a new powerful spell or ritual. People told me it happened to her a lot more often before I was born. When she first came to Coventry, it was like a kaleidoscope.

When I was younger, I would get streaks of color in mine. I always thought it was cool. My magic was restrained, though, so it never made all of my hair change.

Returning to Coventry as an adult must have snapped something loose. My auburn hair had turned a shocking shade of purple. As I watched, the purple blended into a deep turquoise at the ends. It was like that mermaid hair color that women paid hundreds of dollars for except I didn't have to bleach or color mine. It had just happened.

"That's so weird," I said as I walked out of the bathroom.

"I think it suits you, sweetie,," Dad said.

"Thanks," I said. "I guess there's nothing I can do anyway."

"Let's get pancakes," my mom said. "I could really go for some pancakes."

"A trip to the diner?" my dad asked.

"I don't really have money to eat out," I said.

Both of my parents just stared at me like I had two heads. My mother spoke up first.

"We're not asking you to buy your own dinner. We offered. Please, let us take you to dinner?"

"Isn't that what you did on your first night in Coventry?" Dad asked. "I don't think that went well."

"It wasn't my first night, honey. Besides, it's not like we're going to find a dead body."

"You're right," Remy said. "So, what do you say, Kinsley? Welcome home dinner at the diner?"

"Sure," I said. "But what about Meri?"

"I'm fine," he said and started up the stairs. "Just remember to bring me bacon."

"All right, let's go then," I said just as my stomach growled.

I hadn't been eating well because I was trying to make my money last. I couldn't deny that I was starving.

"Sounds like we're just in time," Dad said.

"I guess I'll take my car so you guys don't have to bring me back here after dinner," I said. "I'll just have to get it unhitched from the trailer."

"We'll give you a ride," Mom said.

"Yeah, we can drop you off at home after," Dad said.

My stomach growled again loudly, and I agreed with it. If I rode with my parents, we could get to the diner faster.

"Sure," I said. "Thank you."

Mom and Dad had what looked like a brand new Toyota Camry. It was burgundy and smelled like new car as I slid into the back seat.

"New?" I asked as Dad got behind the wheel.

"We've had it for about a year, but a little magic seals in that new car smell," Mom said.

"We were sorry to hear about the divorce," Dad said as we backed out of the driveway.

"Remy," Mom scolded.

"What? I want her to know we understand and that we're here for her," Dad said.

"Well, we don't need to bring it up tonight," Mom said.

"It's okay, guys. At this point, I'm just glad that it's all over. I'm ready to move on with my life," I said. "Speaking of which, do either of you know of any places around town that are hiring? I'm just about out of cash, and I need to get a job."

"If you make amends, Hangman's House will take care of you, dear," Dad said.

"I know. I remember, but I want to work. I think it's best if I keep busy," I said.

"You could always get married and have grandchildren for your mother and me," Dad said.

"Remy," Mom scolded.

"Ha ha. I'd love to, but I think I need to let the body of my last marriage get cold first," I said.

"Nonsense," Mom said. "We're witches. You can do what you want, but you should probably meet someone first. I'm not sure who your dad is trying to marry you off to."

Dad pulled the car into the parking lot of the diner. It was a new place not far from Hangman's House on the outskirts of town.

"What happened to the old diner?" I asked. "The one near the square."

"It sold to new owners a few years ago, but then they moved out here. With all the tourists, they needed a larger restaurant."

"New tourists?" I asked.

"Yeah, tourism has really picked up in Coventry," Dad said. "Much more so than when people were putting videos of their ghost hunting on YouTube."

"To be fair, one of them died," Mom said. "People dropping dead left and right didn't attract anything other than the strangest of paranormal investigators."

"Tourists, huh?" I asked as my dad parked the car.

"Yeah, why?" Mom asked.

We got out and started walking toward the doors. When we got up there, dad opened the door for my mom and I.

"So, I was thinking of what I could do for work," I said as we waited for the hostess to seat us. "If there are a lot of tourists, then that's room for making a profit."

"You're thinking of opening a business that caters to tourists?" Dad asked. "Like what?"

"I'm not sure, yet," I said. "It's still nebulous."

"Welcome, folks!" a woman dressed in a turquoise dress and white apron said as she walked over to us. As she got closer, I saw that her nametag said Reggie. "Just three this evening?"

"Yes, ma'am," Dad said. "And we'd like a booth if possible."

We sat down and the waitress took our drink order. Dad got a Dr. Pepper and a chocolate milkshake. Mom got a Diet Coke, and I got a regular Coke. I couldn't abide that diet stuff. I didn't know how Mom drank that stuff.

She left and Dad pulled the menus out of the holder between the napkins and the condiment carousel. I opened mine and began to look. The original plan had been for pancakes, but I kinda wanted a burger.

The diner's menu had the perfect solution to my dilemma. They had pancake and sausage sliders with a side of home fries. You could get them with cheese or without, but I wanted mine without cheese so I could dunk them in maple syrup.

"What are you thinking of?" Dad asked.

"I think I want the pancake sliders with a side of syrup," I said.

"That does sound good," he responded.

"Not me, I just want the mega stack," Mom said.

"The mega stack?" I asked.

"Yeah, it's an eight stack," Mom said. "Sometimes they throw a ninth on for free."

"You're going to eat nine pancakes?" I asked.

"Yeah, and a side of cheesy hash browns," Mom said.

"I think that's one of the things I missed most about this place," I said. "I hated having to watch what I ate."

"I hear that," Mom said.

"But why do you drink that diet soda?"

"A habit I picked up before I moved to Coventry," Mom said. "I tried to switch to regular, but it never took."

"What's even weirder is that we've started drinking Coke floats when it's hot, and your Mom puts a scoop of chocolate ice cream in her Diet Coke."

"Oh, gawd, Mom. That's so weird," I said with a laugh.

"What? I like it. That's all that matters, right?"

"Yeah, that's all that matters," I said.

The waitress came and took our orders. When she was gone, we were all quiet for a few minutes. Some of the joy from our reunion had receded, and I knew it was time to start doing the messy work of putting back together what I had broken.

"I can rent a place," I said. "I didn't come here assuming I could stay with you."

That was a lie. I was off to a good start. I didn't know what I was going to do if they didn't let me stay with them, and I certainly didn't have the money to rent a place. If my parents didn't take me in, I was going to have to beg one of my Aunties. Perhaps Aunt Annika and Uncle Gunner would take me in.

"You don't have the money to rent a place," Dad said. "You know your mother and I would never turn you away."

"You don't have to stay with us, though, Kinsley. Hangman's House is yours. I'm not sure how the old house is going to feel about it, but you can make amends. Meri will be glad to be back at the old place," she said with a smile.

"Meri is your familiar, Mom," I protested.

"Meri hasn't been mine since the day you were born. He'll want to stay with you, and I'm not going to stop him."

"What are you going to do for a familiar?" I asked.

"Oh, I'm sure we'll be fine without one. We don't do a ton of magic anymore," Dad said.

"And if we need one, one will come to us," Mom said. "You don't need to worry about that."

I saw the waitress walking across the restaurant toward us with our plates, and my stomach growled loudly. "Sounds like I'm just in time," she said with a chuckle.

"You heard that?" I asked.

"Honey, the whole restaurant heard that, but that's okay. That's what we're here for." She set all of the plates in front of us. "Everything look okay?"

"It does," Dad said.

"Can I get you folks anything else right now?" Reggie asked.

"Not right now," Mom said. "Kinsley?"

"I'm good," I said.

"Kinsley? Kinsley Skeenbauer?" Reggie asked. "I guess that makes sense given who you're with. I haven't seen you in ages!"

I studied her for a moment and tried to place the curly blonde hair and sparkling blue eyes. "Regina Harlow?"

"The one and only." She smiled and gave us a little curtsey. "Are you just visiting, or are you back?"

"I'm back," I said. "I just got back into town today."

"Oh, that's great news. We'll have to catch up soon," Reggie said as the cook rang the bell.

"Hey, Reggie. Order up!" he called from the kitchen.

"I gotta go, but don't be a stranger, okay?"

"I won't," I said.

"She seems nice," Dad said when Reggie walked away. "Where do you know her from?"

"She went to school with me for the time I was there," I said. "Reggie's a nice girl. We had a few classes together. She wasn't one of the girls who picked on me, if that's what you're thinking."

"I don't remember you talking about her," Mom said.

I shrugged. "There was a lot I didn't tell you back then. I forgot that you guys were teenagers once too, and I thought that you'd never understand anything."

"Sounds about right," Dad said. "I felt the same way about my parents."

"There's no way I would have ever told my mother anything," Mom said. "I hope we didn't make you feel like you couldn't talk to us."

"It wasn't you," I said. "It wasn't anything you did or said. Adults just seem like… aliens from another planet at that age. It was like we were different species even."

"That sounds about right too," Dad said with a chuckle.

"Maybe we are aliens," Mom said with a waggle of her eyebrows before shoving a huge forkful of pancake in her mouth.

And just like that, it was like we all understood each other. The sense of relief was instantaneous. I felt tension I didn't even know I had drain from my shoulders. In fact, I felt better than I had in years.

Too bad I had no idea what was in store for me.

Chapter Three

After we were finished with our dinner, Dad paid the bill and we all practically rolled out to the car. "Are you sure I'm not going to get fat?" I asked as I patted my bulging tummy.

I deserved it if I did. I didn't need the slice of blueberry pie a la mode I ate after my pancake sliders, or half of Dad's fries, but I sure did enjoy them.

"You won't gain an ounce," Mom said and patted her stomach. "I mean, you might need to do a little magic occasionally to work it off. You haven't forgotten how, have you?"

"There are some things I think I remember," I said. "It's been a while."

"Well, Dad and I are always here to help you. Meri can assist you too. You've got a whole library in the attic at Hangman's House. Meri can show you any book you need."

"I don't have to start tonight? Do I?" I asked. "I'm tired."

"No, honey. Dad and I will drop you off at home, and you can get some rest. There's still a bed up in one of the spare rooms. You'll find fresh sheets in the hall closet where we always kept them."

"They won't still be fresh, right?"

"Kinsley, honey, they're wrapped in plastic," Dad said. "And if they're not, then just use a little magic. Freshening up some sheets should be easy."

"You're right," I said. "It's going to take some getting used to. I've trained myself to never really think about magic as an option."

"It would probably help if you took that bracelet off," Mom said as we all got into the car.

I'd taken the last bracelet Amelda had ever given me to control my magic and woven it into a new bracelet. Since I'd been a young kid when she gave it to me, it was much too small, but I'd rebraided it with fresh strands and worn it my entire adult life. It wasn't that powerful of a charm, but it did keep me from accidentally popping off some magic.

"Yeah, I should do that," I said. "I'll cut it off when I get back to Hangman's House. I want to keep it. Since it was a gift and all."

"Just don't let Amelda hear you getting all sentimental over it. She'll probably make fun of you and ruin it," Dad said with a chuckle.

"How is my great-grandmother?" I asked.

I worried about Amelda. She had to be pushing one hundred or more. Though, from what my parents had told me over the phone, she didn't seem to get much older anymore, but she did get saltier.

"As sassy as ever. Watch out for the old broad. She might make you think she's going senile, but she's as sharp as a tack. She just wants to keep everyone on their toes, I guess," Mom said with a sigh.

When my parents dropped me off at what was my new home, we kept our goodbyes brief. Still, Dad seemed reluctant to back out of the driveway. Perhaps he was afraid I would slip away in the night again, but that wasn't going to happen. Mom seemed to know that. I waved at them both as they drove away. Mom rolled down her window and waved her arm furiously before blowing me a kiss. Just before they were out of sight, I saw her wink. It was as if she'd known this was where we would end up all along. That helped me feel a little less guilty.

I was through the front door and almost had it locked behind me when I realized I didn't have my purse. It was just a little clutch that I used to carry my wallet, keys, and a tube of lip balm. I'd set it down on the bench next to me at the diner, and I'd forgotten to pick it up again.

"Where are you going?" Meri asked suspiciously when I started back out the door. "Are you really going to pull a runner again so soon?"

"No, I'm not leaving. Well, I'm not leaving Coventry. I left my purse at the diner. I'm going to unhitch the car from the trailer and go get it. Should take me less than fifteen minutes including unhitching the trailer," I said. "You can time me if you want."

"I just might," Meri said as he sauntered off obviously satisfied with my answer.

Once I'd freed my car from the trailer, I backed around it carefully and got out on the road. The diner wasn't far, and when I looked at the clock, I smiled. I was probably going to make it back home in about ten minutes. That would put Meri at ease. I could get my bed ready and pass out. A good night's sleep sounded like just what the doctor ordered.

I parked close to the diner's entrance and I could see my purse sitting next to the cash register. I went inside and almost took it, but I figured I should tell someone first. Otherwise, Reggie might think someone stole it.

But when I looked around, she wasn't there. I waited for a couple of minutes, but my eyes were starting to feel heavy. I just wanted to go home.

When she didn't appear, I walked around to the window where I could see the cook. "Hey, this is my purse. I just wanted to let Reggie know that I took it so she doesn't worry. Can you tell her?"

"Do I look like her secretary?" the cook snarked back at me.

"No... Okay. Do you know where she is?"

"Did you look out back? She said she quit smoking, but some days, I have my doubts," he said and went back to his grill.

I walked back outside and made my way around the building. At first, I thought what I was seeing were some trash bags that someone had left lying on the parking lot. I even said to myself "How lazy can you be not to just throw them in the dumpster?" The dumpster was mere feet away.

I felt frozen in place the moment I realized it was not a pile of garbage bags. An electrical current ran down from my spine to my toes snapping me out of my shock. The pile was in fact, a person, and they might need my help.

"Are you okay?" I asked. "Do you need help?"

I crossed the concrete to the spot where the man had fallen. As I got closer, I could make out for sure that it was a man. I knelt down thinking I was going to maybe give him first aid, but it became immediately obvious that he was already dead. His skin was gray, and pool of blood around him wasn't something anyone could survive. I could also feel that his spirit was gone. It could have been lingering somewhere nearby, but it was no longer in his body.

"What's going on?" Reggie's voice behind me made me jump halfway out of my skin. "Oh, no. Kinsley, what did you do?"

"I didn't do this," I said and stood up.

"Right, of course. It's just that you're kneeling over a dead guy."

"I found him when I came out here looking for you," I said.

"Oh, wow... That's Merrill Killian. That jerk left without leaving me a tip. Again," Reggie said.

"Did you kill him then?" I was half joking. It was probably totally inappropriate timing, but the tension needed to be cut.

"No, I didn't kill him even though he was a stingy old... gentleman," Reggie said, but I could tell *gentleman* was not the word she was thinking. "Was he stabbed?"

"Why do you ask that?"

"There's a bloody knife under the dumpster over there," she said and pointed to it.

"We should call the police," I said.

"Probably go back inside too in case whoever did this is still lurking around somewhere." Reggie crossed her arms over her chest and rubbed the backs of them like she was suddenly cold.

"I'm not worried about that," I said without thinking.

"I knew it! You did kill him," she said and took a step back.

"No, I just..."

I'd let that slip out. I hadn't killed him, of course. The reason I wasn't worried was that I could use magic to protect us, but I couldn't tell Reggie that.

"I'm armed," I said quickly and patted my purse. "I have a concealed carry permit."

"You mean there was a gun in your purse this whole time!" Reggie said. "That's so cool."

"I guess that means you didn't go through it," I said with relief. That little lie could have backfired spectacularly.

"I would never," she said and bit her lower lip. "Okay, I was totally going to, but I had customers. Then I had to get bacon and beef from the freezer. That's where I was when you got here, by the way. Not out smoking like Jimmy said. I really did quit."

"We still haven't called the police."

"I got it," Reggie said and slid her cell phone from her apron.

I surveyed the back portion of the parking area while she was on the phone. I wanted to look around some more, and I was about to walk around the body and walk further past the dumpsters when I saw the ghost of my uncle in the tree line that hugged the edge of the diner parking area.

As Reggie hung up the phone, I ripped the bracelet that limited my powers off my wrist and slid it into my pocket. I didn't think Brody would do anything, but I was prepared to protect myself and Reggie if need be.

"Thorn's on his way," Reggie said. "I should get back inside and check on my customers before the law shows up."

"I'll stand here and make sure none of those customers wander back here and disturb the body," I said.

Reggie narrowed her eyes at me like she was evaluating if I was up to something or not. "Naw, you're not a killer," she said and left.

Thorn's cruiser pulled up a couple of minutes later. He parked close by and then got out. I felt his eyes scan over me. They were narrowed much like Reggie's, and I got the sense I would be evaluated a lot over the next few days. Maybe even longer.

"Breaking and entering and now a dead body?" he asked as he shut the door to his car.

I shrugged. "I guess I bring sunshine and luck with me wherever I go."

Thorn quickly suppressed a chuckle. "Was it you or Reggie that found him?"

He joined me next to the body, Merrill, and checked for himself to see if the guy was dead. Satisfied that he was, Thorn stood up and faced me.

"It was me," I said when I had his attention again. "I found him. I left my purse here at the diner. I came here with my parents. Anyway, I left my purse.

When I came back for it, I found it at the front register. No one was around, though, so I went looking for Reggie. The cook, Jimmy, told me she might be out here. She wasn't, but I found the body."

"Reggie called me, though?" Thorn questioned.

"Yeah, she was in the freezer, I guess. The cook told her he sent me out here. She saw the knife under the dumpster," I said and pointed.

"Did you know him?" Thorn asked.

"No, and I didn't kill him," I said.

"Why would you say that?"

"Because it's what you were thinking," I said.

"How did you know that?"

"Because I found the body," I said. "It's a natural first question. I watch crime shows too."

"I need to tape off the scene and then conduct the investigation," Thorn said as he rubbed the back of his neck. "Where will you be?"

"Uh, I guess I'm living at Hangman's House. I'll be going there when I leave here."

"I'll find you if I have any other questions for you then," Thorn said.

"Why don't I give you my phone number too?" I said. "That way you can call or text if you don't want to come all the way over."

"Very good," Thorn said a little too officially.

"Am I a suspect?" I asked.

"I can't say that you're not right now, but I know your folks pretty well. I have my doubts that they raised a killer. Still, don't leave town," he said.

"Oh, trust me, I don't have anywhere else to go."

Chapter Four

"Where have you been?" Meri came running to the door as soon as I walked into the living room.

"You're not going to believe this, but there was a dead guy behind the diner. I found the body and had to wait for Thorn to let me go," I said.

"Ha ha. You're so stupid," Meri snarked. "That's not even funny."

"I'm not joking," I said deadpan.

"Stop it." Meri's tail was flicking back and forth with agitation. "Where were you really? You said you wouldn't be gone long, and then you were. I thought you bailed again."

"Meri, for real. I found a body behind the diner. Why do you think that's a joke?"

"Wow, okay. I guess Brighton never told you that story," Meri said. "So, when your mom first got to Coventry, she found a body behind the diner. It was the old one, of course. But still, that's so weird."

"That is weird," I said. "But, the universe works in mysterious ways. I can't say I find it that shocking."

"Who was it?" Meri asked.

"Reggie said his name was Merrill Killian," I said and took my first good look around. "Hey, wait a minute.

Where did all this furniture come from? Has the house forgiven me already?"

"Some of the Aunties came by and brought you stuff. I think they planned on seeing you, but you were gone so long that they all wandered off. They'll be back. Probably tomorrow."

"Were they worried that I wasn't back yet?" I asked.

"No, and neither was I," Meri said and sashayed off.

"Whatever," I said after him.

"Whatever."

I went out to the trailer and quickly grabbed a suitcase that had some of my clothes in it and my overnight bag. The master bedroom had been empty when I arrived, but I found it completely furnished when I went upstairs to go to bed.

The four-poster bed sat in the middle of the room on a plush red carpet. There was a large mahogany dresser on one wall and a smaller one on the wall that led into the bathroom. Hangman's House had been remodeled at some point when I was very little, and the largest upstairs bedroom had been turned into a master suite. At least, I thought that's what my mother had said. The first floor and the upstairs attic had been left alone, though.

I took my overnight bag into the bathroom and dropped it as soon as I walked in. "You've got to be kidding me," I said and quickly flipped on the light.

My parents did not have a stone walk-in shower and clawfoot tub in their bathroom when I left, but there it was right before my eyes. There was also a long vanity with dual sinks. The stone sink basins looked like bowls sitting atop soapstone counters that coordinated with the showers. The faucets were open on the top and when I turned it on, it created a mini waterfall into the basin.

"They got pretty fancy," Meri said as he wandered into the room.

"And then they left all of this?" I said.

"Your mom wanted a new project," Meri said. "So, they moved into Remy's old place and she started fancying that house up. She took a lot more liberties in there because she wasn't worried about the historical value of the house."

"She needed a project," I said. "Because I was gone?"

"Don't get started on that. Just get ready for bed," Meri said. "You'll have plenty of time to feel bad about running out on your family later."

"Thanks," I said.

"No problem."

I took my toothbrush and toothpaste out of my bag and set them on the counter. I'd just planned on brushing my teeth and going to bed, but the stone shower with gigantic rainfall shower head was practically calling my name.

After a couple of minutes, the bathroom was filled with steam. I stepped inside and sighed with relief as the hot water washed my day away.

And then I screamed as the water turned ice cold. I practically fell trying to navigate the wet stone to get out of the shower, and I knew I came close to breaking my head or my butt.

"What is it?" Meri came running, but when he saw me standing there trying to get a towel wrapped around me, he turned away. "My eyes!!!"

"Oh, shut up," I said.

"What happened?" he asked.

"The water turned ice cold," I said as my teeth chattered. "It happened so fast, it shocked me. That's why I screamed."

"Well, either the water heater went out or there's a ghost, and I don't sense a ghost," Meri said. "Probably just the house's way of saying hello."

"Does Coventry have a plumber that does after-hours emergency calls?"

"Do you have soap in your hair?" Meri asked.

"No, why?"

"Because you don't really need an emergency plumber if you don't. Why pay triple the fee when you can just wait until tomorrow?'"

"What if the pilot light is out? It could explode."

"Your parents had it upgraded to one of those new jobbies with the safety pilot light. It can't explode. You need to chill," he said. "Sorry, poor choice of words."

"I think I'd like to check for myself," I said.

"It's in the basement," Meri answered.

"I've never been in the basement," I said. "Mom and Dad worried I'd wander into the tunnels and get lost."

"Well, you won't now. There's a locking door you have to go through to access them now. You can't accidentally stumble into them anymore. And even if you do go into them, they have electricity with lights and everything."

"Do people even use them?" I asked.

"No. Not really. Everyone has doors on their access points and they just keep them locked all of the time."

"Where do they go? I've heard they go outside of Coventry."

"Do you want to look at the water heater? Or do you want to stand here in your bathroom yammering about tunnels?"

"Let me get dressed, and I'll meet you in the kitchen."

"Whatever," he said and left.

I threw on the sweat pants and t-shirt that would serve as my pajamas. Figuring it would be chilly down there, I also pulled my favorite cardigan out of my suitcase. I couldn't sleep in long sleeves, but most of the time, I needed them when I was milling around the house.

My hair was cold and wet, so I tied it up in a bun and dried the back of my neck a second time. After slipping on a dingy pair of sneakers I kept for just such occasions, I went down to the kitchen to meet Meri.

"When I was younger, my friends told me I wasn't allowed down in the basement because Mom and Dad kept powerful magic stuff down there," I said I opened the basement door.

"Yeah, but not so much anymore," Meri said. "Anything dangerous got moved to the other house. They actually finished the basement as a part of the remodel thing Brighton did. There is a storage room down there, though. It's got lots of stuff in it. Just nothing that's super dangerous."

"Stuff?" I asked as we descended the stairs.

"Herbs, crystals, candles. Stuff like that. There are some spell books and a few shelves of premade potions too," Meri said. "I think there are a few cases of Diet Coke as well."

We got to the bottom of the steps, and I flipped on the light. The basement was not what I was expecting at all. The dirty, gray stone floor that I'd remembered seeing once when my dad had left the door open had been replaced by warm terracotta tiles. When I stepped into the main area, there was a bar with black leather stools. Behind the bar was a small refrigerator, a two-burner stovetop, pizza oven, and a microwave. On the other side of the large room was an area with a huge leather sectional sofa and a big screen television hanging on the wall.

"Did the Aunties put this stuff here?" I asked.

"Nope. Your parents didn't take it with them because they haven't finished the basement at the new house yet."

"You could throw quite the party down here."

"That was the idea. Your Mom thought about using it for entertaining," Meri said. "Follow me."

He walked to the other side of the basement where there was a turn into another section. There were four doors. One was to my left, two to my right, and the one straight ahead in a brick wall.

"I take it that's the one that goes into the tunnels?" I said and pointed to the one in the brick wall. It had several heavy locks on it.

"Yep," Meri answered.

The door to my left was open, and I could see inside. It was a small guest bathroom.

"And these two?" I said and walked over to the doors on the right.

"This one is the witch pantry," Meri said and walked past the first one. "This is the utility closet."

Inside the utility closet was a sump pump, a new-looking furnace, and an even newer-looking water heater. At first, I wasn't sure there even was a water heater in the utility room because they'd installed one of those tankless instant models. It was up off the floor on the wall, and Meri was right. It even said on the side of it in big letters that it was operated by a safety pilot light. There was a little window that allowed me to look inside and see that it was lit.

"Why did you do that?" I asked the house. "It wasn't very nice."

Just then the lights went out in the basement and I was left standing in nearly pitch-black darkness. The only light at all was the tiny glow from the pilot light window.

"Good job," Meri said.

"Sorry," I said. "Illuminae."

An orb of light appeared in front of me, and it stayed there as I exited the utility room.

"That was pretty good," Meri said. "I could have done that too."

"But you didn't. You just groused."

"Whatever."

"I think I'm going to go to bed now," I said. "Maybe the water heater will be working again in the morning."

"You could always use magic," Meri said.

"I don't know. It seems safer to maybe call a plumber."

"That's not going to work if it's just the house being mean to you."

"Okay fine. If it's still not working in the morning, I'll try. My confidence in doing anything other than this orb isn't high, though."

The orb of light I'd conjured lit our way back upstairs. I was pleased to find the power still on in the kitchen, and with a wave of my hand, the light orb disintegrated into a wisp.

Bone-deep fatigue gripped me at that point, and all I wanted to do was fall into my new bed. Meri followed me upstairs, and I climbed into the king-size four-poster bed. The sheets were fresh and had the lightest scent of lavender.

I grabbed my phone from my purse and set an alarm for six the next morning. I didn't have any reason to get up early other than I wanted to be prepared for whatever the day brought me.

Just before I set the phone down, I got a text message from a number I didn't recognize.

Hey, Kinsley. This is Thorn. I just wanted to make sure you got home safe.

"That's interesting," I said to Meri. He'd curled up next to me on the bed already.

"I doubt it, but what?" Meri asked.

"Thorn just texted me to make sure I got home safe," I said and started to respond.

"Figures," Meri said. "I hope that one is smarter than his father."

"What?"

"Never mind."

"Okay."

I did. Thank you for checking in. I typed. I wasn't sure what else to say. It felt like I should say something else, but it escaped me. *Good night.* That seemed okay.

Good night. Let me know if you need anything.

I was just about to respond again when Meri interrupted.

"Don't you dare text him back again. Leave him hanging," Meri suggested.

"That seems rude."

"You told him you made it home safe. Leave him wanting more."

"For what? Wanting more what?"

"Just put the phone down and go to sleep, Kinsley. Trust me here."

I really, really, really wanted to text Thorn back again, but I decided to listen to Meri. He was my familiar after all, and it was his job to protect me. He wouldn't lead me astray.

I hoped.

Chapter Five

The next morning, I was awakened by the sensation of Meri licking my eye. "Oh, gawd. Meri! What are you doing?"

I reached for my phone and it was an hour before my alarm was due to go off.

"I'm hungry," Meri said.

"What? You woke me up because you want breakfast?" I asked. "It's five in the morning."

"I'm a cat. What do you want?" Meri said and jumped off the bed. "Oh, and the bathroom is flooded."

"What?"

I sat straight up in bed and looked over. Sure enough, there was a half inch of standing water in the bathroom and it was soaking into the carpet.

I scrambled out of bed and stomped through the water into the bathroom. The rain shower head was on full blast, and there was the towel I dropped covering the drain.

When I pulled the towel out of the way of the drain, the water started to go down, but very slowly. I reached up to turn the water off, and the knob just spun.

"No. No. No," I said as the water continued to gush out of the shower head. It was coming out with such force that the pipe was actually vibrating. I was afraid it was going to burst.

I wracked my brain trying to remember if there had been a toolbox in the utility room in the basement, or if I'd seen one anywhere else. Then I remembered that I had no idea how to fix plumbing, and I might make everything worse.

"Use magic, genius," Meri said.

He was sitting in the bedroom watching me from the doorway. Well, not exactly the doorway. He'd had to move a foot or so back to avoid the wet carpet. If I didn't do something fast, I was going to have a huge disaster on my hands.

"Enough," I said.

The water from the shower head stopped, and I heard the drain gurgle to life.

I rubbed my hands over my face and calmly walked over to the sink. As the freezing cold water drained away from my feet, the drain opening was low enough since it was an open shower that the entire bathroom could clear, I brushed my teeth.

"Dry," I said as I put my toothbrush in the holder, and the wetness dissipated from the carpet instantly. "Let's get some breakfast, and I'm calling a plumber later."

Meri wanted salmon, which I found in the fridge. I wanted eggs, which there were none of. I closed the refrigerator door and opened the freezer. Inside there, I found pancake and sausage on a stick things that I liked when I was a kid.

"Do you think these are poison?" I asked Meri as I pulled two out.

"I think the house probably thinks you've had enough for today," Meri said.

Sure enough, when I opened the fridge again, there was a carton of free-range eggs from a local farm on the top shelf.

"Thank you," I said to the house. "Thank you so much for these."

Since Meri acted like he was starving, I got his breakfast first. Once he was fed, I put on a pot of coffee and got a skillet. They were in the same place my mother had kept them when this was still her house. One more trip to the fridge netted me some butter. I clicked on the stove, put the skillet on the burner, and cut a tablespoon of butter from the stick. After it plopped into the pan, I stood there and watched it melt.

As soon as I cracked my eggs into the pan, the doorbell rang. "What?" I asked no one in particular.

It was early, and I hoped it wasn't any of my family already. I was expecting to see them that day, but I needed more time to prepare.

The doorbell rang again.

"All right, okay," I said. "I'm coming!" I called out.

I opened the door ready to lay into whoever was ringing my bell so early, and found Thorn standing on my front porch. He was dressed in jeans and a gray sweater that accentuated his large, muscular arms. "I know it's early. I'm sorry," he said. "I'm about to start my shift, and I wanted to talk to you before I got busy."

"It's okay," I said. "Come in. I've got coffee going, and I'm making eggs."

"Oh, I can grab coffee and a stale donut at the station," Thorn said as he stepped inside. "I'm not here to impose."

"It's no imposition at all. Let me throw a couple more eggs in the pan," I said. "If you're here, and we're going to talk about police business, then you might as well eat too."

"Are you sure?" Thorn asked.

"I wouldn't have offered if I wasn't," I said. "We could have talked on the porch."

Thorn followed me into the kitchen and grabbed a coffee mug from the cabinet. He'd spent some time in Hangman's House. That was apparent. "Sorry if I'm being rude," he said suddenly realizing that I wasn't my mother.

"It's okay. Pour yourself a cup and have a seat. I'll have these eggs ready in just a few minutes."

"Oh, I used to love those when I was a kid," Thorn said as he eyed the pancake and sausage on a stick I'd pulled from the freezer.

I was a little embarrassed that he'd seen me, a grown woman, getting ready to eat them, but he looked so happy that I decided to go with it.

"Well, then I guess what we're having with our eggs is settled," I said. "Go sit down, I'll bring the food over in a second."

"You don't have to wait on me," Thorn said.

"I'm not," I responded. "But, you're a guest in my house, so you sit and I serve. I know it's long since out of fashion for a woman to serve a man his breakfast, but I don't mind doing things the old way sometimes."

"I think there are some feminists who would have an issue with that," he said, but there wasn't any mocking or distaste in his voice.

I laughed. "I know, but feminism means doing what I choose. I choose to serve my guest breakfast. Now, scoot out of my kitchen before I take a spatula to your rear," I said playfully.

And then my face turned as red as a beet. Not only had I just shamelessly flirted with him, but I'd been more forward than I'd ever been with a man. I barely knew him. Sure, it sort of felt like we'd known each other forever, but in reality, I'd met him the night before when he thought I was breaking into the very house where we were about to have breakfast together.

"I..." I stammered and couldn't get any more words out.

"Ha ha. You're trouble," he said and walked over to the table and sat down. "Is this far enough away?"

There was a row of upper and lower cabinets with an open counter in between the main part of the kitchen and the breakfast nook. The cabinets acted as sort of a half or three-quarter wall between the areas, but you could still see the people on either side. It was technically still in the kitchen but technically out too.

"I suppose," I said.

"So, what brings you back to Coventry?" Thorn asked in between tentative sips of his coffee.

"Divorce," I said flatly. "But I presume you're just being polite asking and my mother has already told you all about it."

"I wouldn't say all about it," Thorn responded. "You married a high school sweetheart or something. I know you didn't go to regular high school all four years."

"Yeah, I had to leave school and do an online school instead because... I had some issues at the school."

"You mean you gave some mean girls the what for," Thorn said.

"You know about that?" I felt heat rising in my cheeks again.

"Yeah, and this is going to shock you, but I know it was magic and not some chemistry lab experiment gone wrong like the official story says," he said and winked at me.

"Wait, you know..."

"Worst-kept secret in all of Coventry," Thorn said.

"Did my mother tell you?"

"No, my dad did," Thorn said and rubbed his chin. "He told me right before he passed. Sort of a deathbed confession. It ate at him his whole life what he left behind. At first, I thought it was just his mind going out because of all of the drugs and chemo stuff, but after he was gone, I felt drawn to this place. It was like an insatiable itch I couldn't scratch, so I applied to be a deputy. The rest, I guess, is history."

"Your father died of cancer? My mother didn't heal him?" I couldn't believe it.

"He didn't tell her," Thorn said. "He couldn't bring himself to come back here begging for her help after the way he left her. I wish he had.'"

"If she'd known," I said.

"I know. She said the same thing," Thorn said. "It's been a long time."

"I'm sorry."

"I'd like to say that we don't have to talk about such dark things, but I actually came here to talk to you about something just as dark," Thorn said.

"Why don't we eat first," I said. I plated the food and took it over to the table. "One more thing."

I went to the pantry and got a bottle of maple syrup. There were small red ramekins right where I remembered them, so I poured Thorn and I each a serving of syrup for dipping our pancakes and sausage on a stick.

I sat down to eat, and Thorn tore into his. "This is so much better than the horrible coffee at the station and stale donuts," he said. "Thank you."

"You don't look like you eat a lot of junk food," I said and realized that probably sounded really flirtatious.

It was the truth, but I was being overly forward again. I couldn't help it, though. I just seemed unable to hold back around Thorn.

You just got divorced. I reminded myself. I'd sworn off relationships for good when my ex-husband and I split, but I found myself wondering if I'd been too hasty. I didn't know Thorn, but he was handsome. And I could tell he was kind. If there were men like him out there, then perhaps I shouldn't write love off. *Jeez, Kinsley. You just met the guy yesterday.*

"Penny for your thoughts?" Thorn asked when he finished the last of his food.

"I was just wondering who might have killed that Merrill Killian guy," I lied, but I was not going to tell him my real thoughts. *I was thinking about how your biceps are so spectacular that they made me believe in love again.*

"Well, I guess since we're done eating, we might as well dive into that," Thorn grimaced.

"Did you come here to tell me I'm not a suspect anymore, because that would be great."

"Unfortunately not, but I still don't think it was you. So I won't be investigating it that way, but you need to be wary. You're new in town, so people are going to think it was you."

"I'm not really new in town," I countered. "I did grow up here."

"Yeah, and you slipped out in the middle of the night when you were seventeen and broke your parents' hearts. That's going to be enough for some people to decide your guilt alone."

"That was kind of rude," I said and felt myself bristle. "I guess it's fair, though."

"Hey, I understand. If my dad hadn't adopted me, I probably would have gone down a totally different path in life," Thorn said.

"Wait, what?" I couldn't believe what I was hearing.

"Yeah, Thorn wasn't my biological father," he said.

"You sound like you look just like what my mother said Thorn looked like," I said.

"My mother had a type," Thorn said with a shrug. "That's why my dad thought he was my bio dad for so long. It was a shock when he found out he wasn't. I'd just started kindergarten."

"Wow," I said.

"He didn't leave my mom when he found out. He swallowed his pride and stayed for me and my sister. My biological father signed away his rights to me, and Thorn adopted me immediately. Later, when my mom left him, he got custody of us kids. It wasn't always easy, but he made it work. I'm sorry. I have no idea why I'm dumping all of this on you. We just met, and I'm vomiting out some pretty personal stuff," he said and straightened his back.

"It's okay. I don't mind at all."

"It always felt like I could just talk to your mom. I really shouldn't act like you are the same person, though."

"In a lot of ways, we are a lot alike," I said.

"Headstrong," Thorn observed. "I get the feeling you're both good people too. Well, I know your mother is. I mean that I get the same feeling about you."

"Even though I ran off and broke my parents' hearts?" I asked.

"You came back when you were ready," he said. "A lot of people wouldn't. My bio dad wouldn't."

"I didn't have much choice," I said. "My ex got me fired from my job and left me broke. He was a real gem."

"Well, there aren't many job openings in a town this small, but I'm sure there's something."

"I was thinking of starting a business. I know that sounds crazy because I just said I was broke, but I'm trying to think of a way."

"There's a shop on the square that's for rent. It's super cheap because the place is supposed to be really haunted," Thorn said.

"I'll have to go check that out," I said.

"Maybe wait until things blow over?" Thorn offered.

"I'm just going to go look," I said. "I promise I won't cause any trouble."

"You sure you can keep that promise?" It was playful, but there was still an edge to his voice.

"I'll do my best," I said. "But, you said you came here to discuss the case?"

"I'm not sure that I said that exactly," Thorn said. "One thing I wanted to do was get a look at your hands, and I've done that."

"My hands?"

"The victim was stabbed. You wouldn't believe how often the person doing the stabbing accidentally cuts themselves."

"Well, are you satisfied, then?" I said.

"Mostly, but we both know you could heal yourself," Thorn countered.

"Not for personal gain," I said. "I mean, I guess technically I could, but there would be consequences."

"I understand that. But with that being said, I was hoping you would give a blood sample and some DNA. It will help rule you out."

"Don't you need a court order for that?" I asked.

"Unless you volunteer."

"But it will rule me out?" I asked.

"Especially if we find the killer's blood at the scene and it's not yours," he said.

"Okay, when, where, and how?"

"I can meet you at the clinic this afternoon. One of the nurses can take the samples, and I'll take them into evidence."

"All right. Let's do that then," I said.

Chapter Six

Thorn left, and I decided to take another chance at a shower. This time, the pipes cooperated. Since the house didn't attack me with cold water again and my magic had worked, I decided to hold off on the plumber.

What Thorn had said about a space being for rent in the square had piqued my interest. Especially since he said it would be cheap. Checking it out was also an excuse to get out of the house and possibly avoid a huge welcome home party.

At least for a while anyway.

I dried my hair and dug my favorite pair of jeans and black sweater out of my bag. I never wore much makeup, but I wanted to look presentable, so I pulled my makeup case out. While I was putting on mascara, it hit me that neither Thorn nor Reggie had said anything about my hair. Reggie hadn't seen me when I came into town, so maybe she just assumed it was my look.

Thorn, on the other hand had seen me before my mermaid transformation. I'd had it pulled up, so maybe it wasn't that noticeable. Or perhaps he just wasn't the type to make comments on a woman's hair. Especially when he'd come over to see if I had cuts on my hands because I'd stabbed some guy behind the diner. He hadn't said anything the night before either. I figured he'd probably say something later. Especially if it changed again, and he didn't have a murder case to solve.

I thought about putting my hair in a bun again to try to hide the color, but some women paid hundreds of dollars to look that way. I did tie it up in a high ponytail though so that the color could cascade down my back. A little bit of turquoise eye shadow and a slick of nude gloss completed the look. For a moment, I thought about how my ex-husband would have busted something if he saw me with that hair and wearing turquoise eye shadow, but I brushed those thoughts aside and headed downstairs.

"Where are you going?" Meri asked as I slid my feet into my black boots.

"Down to the square to look at that shop Thorn was talking about," I said as I sat on the stairs to tie the laces. "I know you heard him."

"He also said to wait until you're not a murder suspect anymore," Meri said.

"I'm just going to have a look," I said.

"I'm going with you," Meri countered.

"Fine."

"Whatever."

I grabbed my purse and we headed out to the car. it was a short drive down to the square, and I pulled my hunk of junk into a parking spot between two shiny, silver self-driving cars. It was a little strange seeing the ultra-modern vehicles parked outside of the old historic buildings around the square. I walked across the square past the statues of my family members. A hum vibrated in my chest as I crossed the ley line and it connected with the magic inside me.

It was almost enough to make me stop, but I was on a mission. I could see the vacant shop with a "for rent" sign in the window. Meri was walking along next to me, and I thought I'd get some weird looks for that, but no one paid him any mind.

We passed a small group of tourists who were listening to their guide tell a story about a ghost in the courthouse. I didn't hear much of it because I was walking quickly, but what I did catch was that the ghost was a woman in white with black holes for eyes and a mouth. A woman in the group quickly covered her child's ears and I had to chuckle. What had she expected to hear on a ghost tour of Coventry? At least, I assumed that's what it was. I'd seen similar small walking tours in other towns I'd visited.

There was a little traffic, but I crossed the street and Meri and I stood in front of the vacant shop. "This place is too haunted for this town?" I asked.

Meri didn't respond other than with a flick of his tail. There were too many normal people and tourists around for him to talk.

I stepped closer and leaned in using my hands to cover the sides of my eyes so I could see inside. It was dusty, but I could tell it had previously been a lovely store. I was thinking books based on the wood shelves lining the walls and arranged in the center. I could vaguely remember there being a book store there in the past as well. It had been owned by the man who ran the defunct Coventry Historical Society. He'd opened the store when he bought a bunch of rare books at an auction for super cheap. I wondered what had happened to him and his store. Not enough to really ask anyone. He'd been an unpleasant man.

But, had ghosts run him out of business? From what I knew, the Coventry Historical Society was a cover for the Coventry Paranormal Society. Ghosts couldn't have run the leader of a paranormal society out of business, right?

There was a number on the "for rent" sign. I pulled my phone out of my purse and dialed. I felt Meri's claw tugging at my pant leg. When I looked down, he was glaring at me. If he could talk, he probably would have said something about how I'd said we were just looking.

"I'm still just looking," I said to him.

"Excuse me?" Someone had picked up on the other end of the phone.

"Oh, sorry. Not you," I said. "Hello, I'm Kinsley Skeenbauer, I'm interested in renting the shop in the Coventry Town Square."

"It's haunted," the voice on the other end grumbled.

"I know. That's why I want to rent it," I said a little too enthusiastically.

"Really?"

"Yes."

"Are you there now?" the man asked.

"I am. I'm standing out front."

"Be there in five," he said and the line went dead.

"He said he'd be here in five minutes," I said as I slid the phone back into my purse.

I looked around to see where the little ghost tour had moved onto and noticed there was a woman standing across the street staring at me. She was dressed in a bright red, below-the-knee dress with huge white flowers on it. Her graying dishwater blonde hair was pulled back in a severe bun that stretched the sides of her eyes. Even from across the street, I thought it looked painful. *Maybe that's why she's staring daggers at me,* I reasoned. She probably had one heck of a headache.

"Can I help you?" I shouted across the street when she didn't look away.

"Are you nuts?" Meri chanced a whisper.

A car passed right as he said it, so there was no way anyone else heard. "She's freaking me out." I whispered when I knelt down and pretended to tie my boot lace. "You can see her, right? She's not, like, a ghost?"

"No, she's real, and she's walking across the street so stop talking to me."

I stood up and suddenly the woman was toe to toe with me. "Are you here to show me the shop?" I asked.

Maybe I'd misread her and the voice on the phone.

"No, and I hope the landlord doesn't rent this place to the likes of you. That's all we need is trash like you littering up our beautiful downtown area," she snarled.

"Excuse me?" I hadn't misread her.

"You heard me. I don't know what kind of vile business you're planning on opening here, but it's not welcome in Coventry. Neither are you. We haven't had a murder in years. Not until the spawn of that other troublemaker rolled into town. You need to keep on rolling."

Her breath smelled like garlic and eggs. I took a step back. One, so I didn't have to smell it and two, I was fighting the urge to clock her.

"Don't talk about my mother," I practically growled.

I could feel heat rising up from my chest into my face. My vision began to narrow as rage filled me. It was a rage that had been building up inside of me since I'd found out my ex-husband wanted a divorce, and it was all about to be channeled at this unfortunate woman on the street. If I were a dragon, I'd have burned her alive right there for all of the tourists to see.

But instead, I felt Meri rub against my legs. A tingle ran up them until it reached my heart. My muscles relaxed, and my heart rate slowed. The rage dialed itself down into a simmer like a boiling pot pulled off the stove and placed on the cooler back burner. My vision widened back to normal, and I took a deep, cleansing breath.

"Don't talk about my mother," I said again, but in a far more polite tone. "You'd be wise to leave my family out of this."

"Why do you care?" the woman sniped. "The word is that you ran away from home when you were just a surly teenager. If you ask me, we were all better off without you."

"Do I know you?" I asked as calmly as I could.

I was determined at that point not to give the woman the satisfaction of riling me up, but I had to find a way to get rid of her before the landlord showed up. Only the goddess knew why I hadn't abandoned the idea of opening a shop at that point. It was obvious that doing so would cause me immense trouble.

"I doubt it," she said. "Doesn't matter who I am anyway. What matters is that you pack that trailer up and roll on outta here with your crappy car and even crappier trouble."

Before I could respond, the woman turned and left. She hurried back across the street without looking and was nearly taken out by a car full of teenagers. She made it safely, though, and I watched her walk down the square. A minute later, the woman disappeared behind the courthouse.

"Kinsley Skeenbauer?" a voice asked from behind me.

I turned to find a man with dark olive skin and gray hair. He had tiny black-rimmed spectacles perched on the end of his long nose and was dressed in chocolate brown pants and a matching vest. Under that, he wore a faded blue cotton dress shirt.

"Nice to meet you, Mr..." I said and stuck out my hand.

He took it. "It's Mr. Andino. Castor Andino."

"Thank you for meeting me, Mr. Andino."

"Are you still interested in the place?"

I thought it was an odd question as we'd just spoken minutes before. It would have been very peculiar for me to change my mind already.

"Why would I have changed my mind already?" I asked.

"I'm guessing you looked through the window?" He flinched like I was going to slap him.

"I did. It's a lovely store. That's why I called," I said. "I'd like to take a look around inside."

"Oh, okay. Most people aren't interested anymore by the time I get here.'"

"Really?" I asked. "Why is that?"

"I don't want to put ideas that aren't there in your head," he responded.

"Because it's supposed to be haunted, I offered.

"It *is* haunted."

"Even so..." I started but he cut me off.

"I'd feel bad even renting the place to you," Castor said and shoved his hands in his pocket.

"For what I'd want to use the building for, the haunting would be a feature, not a bug."

"I can't imagine how that could be possible," he said.

"Well, there seems to be a lot of new tourism in Coventry since I left, and I'd like to capitalize on that. I was thinking of opening an occult store. Something witchy to take advantage of the vibe in town."

"Oh," Castor said, but he sounded more intrigued than put off. I took that as a good sign.

"So, can I see it?" I asked.

"Sure. Sure," he said and started to unlock the door. "But you'll have to go in alone. I'd, uh... I'd rather stay out here."

"You're not going to come in and show me around?" I asked.

"I think you can figure it out. There's a front room, back room, small office, and a bathroom. I'll wait out here," Castor said.

"Okay," I said.

Castor held the door for me, and I scooped Meri up into my arms. I walked inside the shop and immediately felt a heaviness. I almost turned back right then and there, but took a step forward instead.

The door closed behind me, and as soon as it did, Meri spoke up. "You can feel that, right?"

"Yeah, but it's not that bad," I said. "If this place is cheap, we can deal with it."

"Kinsley," Meri said. "Nobody is going to buy anything in this atmosphere. You'd be wasting your time and money."

"If I was a mere human I would be," I said. "But we can take care of this. We'll cleanse whatever is causing it. Don't you want to go explore?"

"No, I'll stay here with you for now."

"Don't tell me you're scared of a little ghost? Meri, the great demon hunter? Please give me a break."

"I'm not scared. I just don't know where that's coming from yet. I'll stay here with you until we do."

"Whatever floats your boat," I said with a shrug.

Despite the slightly oppressive feeling in the air, the shop was nice. The lighting was just right for a cozy yet mystical feeling once we got rid of the disgruntled spirit. Towards the back of the front area of the store was a wood display case with a glass front. A cash register sat on top of it, and I thought that was a cool perk. I wouldn't have to buy a register to use in the store. I wouldn't even have known where to buy a cash register, but I figured probably on the internet.

Behind that was a door that led into the back area of the store. Off to the left was the small office. I went inside and turned on the light. There wasn't much in there, but it was furnished with a desk and an office chair. I had a laptop that I could bring in from home until I could afford to buy a computer just for the shop. I turned off the light, stepped out of the office, and closed the door behind me.

I heard a faint rattling coming from the door up ahead to the right. "Maybe it's just a pipe," I said to Meri who was still at my feet. "That should be the bathroom."

"Yeah, maybe it's just the pipes," Meri agreed, but his voice was mocking.

"Well, even if it is a ghost, if the haunting is only in the back, then it's not going to be a problem. Even if we couldn't get rid of it, which we can, customers aren't going to care what goes on back here," I said and waved my arms to indicate the rows of metal shelves used for stock.

The rattling sound in the room switched to being a light tapping on the door. Whatever was inside was knocking like it wanted to get out, but it was very faint. I found it more unnerving than if it had been pounding on the wooden door.

"Maybe it's just rats," Meri snarked.

I rolled my eyes at his sass. "Hey, whatever you are... whoever you are... you might as well show yourself. We're not scared. You're wasting your time trying to intimidate us. Not that you're short on that. You're dead after all," I called out.

The knocking stopped, and it was followed by a faint squeaking sound. At first, I couldn't figure out what the heck it was. Then it dawned on me. It was like the sound of someone raking their hand down the glass mirror that was probably in the bathroom.

"Very clever," I said. "But still not going to work."

I started walking toward the bathroom door. The specter wasn't going to come out, so the only solution was to go in. I assumed the ghost wasn't dangerous, like the spirit of my Uncle Brody, because they couldn't be a witch. Surely, a powerful ghost wouldn't resort to making creepy noises behind a closed door. Such things were below the more potent dead.

When I put my hand on the knob, it turned icy cold. Not enough to actually hurt me, but enough to startle me and make me draw my hand back. The sensation faded from my fingers quickly, and I reached out to grasp the knob again. That time, I used a little fire magic to keep my hand warm.

Unfortunately, while I was paying attention to the ghost in the bathroom, I wasn't paying any mind to what was going on behind me. Neither was Meri as he sat dutifully at my feet staring up at the door. He was in position to pounce on whatever was inside. I'd hate for him to have had to blow up a demon inside the shop I wasn't even renting yet, but he would have if necessary.

I heard the creaking sound of someone pushing the metal shelving behind me over right before the edge slammed into the back of my head. Meri must have used magic to catch it because right after it cracked into my skull, it lifted off me. My vision went black before I could focus enough to use a healing spell and I slumped to the floor. I felt myself falling, but I did not feel my body and head hit the bare concrete floor beneath me.

When I opened my eyes, Meri was pawing at my face. He was about to lick my eyelid when I stopped him. "Whoa, no need to get weird. I'm awake," I said. "Thanks for healing me."

"Don't thank him yet," a voice said from behind Meri.

"That's the ghost that tried to kill you," Meri said. "I cast a circle around us, so he can't get in, but unfortunately, I can't banish him."

"What? Why not?"

"Unfinished business," Meri said with a sigh. "He has unfinished business, and because of that, the magic to banish him won't work."

I looked over at the ghost. "It's the man from behind the diner," I said. "Merrill Killian. Wait, why is he haunting this shop?"

"He's not the ghost that was messing around in the bathroom," Meri said. "Merrill isn't haunting the shop. He's haunting you."

"You can get rid of me easy." Merrill's ghost said. "Just bring my killer to justice."

"Well, that will be easier with you here," I said. "So, who killed you? I'll be happy to tell the sheriff."

"I don't know," he said and my heart sank.

"Wait, what? You were stabbed through the heart. How could you not know who did it? Were they wearing a mask?" I asked.

"I can't remember the day I died." Merrill said. "In order to bring my killer to justice, you're going to have to figure out who it is."

"Great," I said. "I mean, I can do that but not if you keep trying to kill me."

"Yeah, I guess I'm sorry about that. It's just that I keep getting so angry. I don't know where it comes from. I wasn't a patient man in life, but I never tried to thump a woman on the head with a metal shelf."

"You're a vengeful spirit," Meri said matter-of-factly. "Not knowing who killed you is only going to make it worse."

"That sounds awesome," I said sarcastically.

"He's only going to get more dangerous and more violent the longer it takes to find his killer," Meri said. "And we can't banish him. Not without some serious ritual stuff that you might not be into."

I turned back to Merrill and noticed that he was starting to fade away. The dead could only hang on for so long. He would run out of strength to show himself to us soon, and he'd probably used up a lot of his energy knocking that shelf over on me. Once he slipped away, there was no telling how long it would be before he returned. I had the sinking feeling that when he did come back, he'd return with even more rage than this time.

"We're losing you, Merrill. Pretty soon, you won't be able to interact with the living again until you gain some strength back. So, if you want me to solve your murder, you have to give me something to go off of before that happens. I know you can't remember the day you died, but can you remember the rest of your life?"

"Almost as well as when I was still breathing," he said.

"All right then, who do you think killed you? You must know somebody that would have reason."

"I gave a lot of people reasons." He scratched the five o'clock shadow he died with on his chin. "None probably as much as my ex-wife. I ruined her life good," he said with a chuckle that made my stomach turn.

Before I could ask him anything else, like his ex-wife's name, Merrill started to fade even more. He moved his mouth like he was saying something, but there was no sound. As soon as he was gone, the tapping on the bathroom door started again.

"Can it," I said. "I'm not in the mood for your shenanigans and you're not going to scare me off either. I've got bigger problems to deal with."

The tapping turned into scratching. Meri trotted over to the door and waited for me to open it.

"If you're not gone when I open this door, we're going to banish you," I said and reached for the knob. "You'd better scram unless you're ready to go to the other side."

The noise stopped, and I opened the door. Inside, all I found was a small bathroom with a dingy white linoleum floor and old, but clean, white porcelain commode and sink. I turned on the light to have a better look. There was toilet paper on the roll and across from the commode was a locker cabinet with two lockers. I stepped inside the bathroom and opened those. Inside was extra stock of paper towels, toilet paper, and bottles of hand soap. Whoever had rented the shop before had left it all behind.

I switched off the light and shut the door. "I guess it's time to go," I said to Meri. "Unless there's something else you want to see."

"No, I've seen enough," he groused. "You're going to rent this place, though, aren't you?"

"As long as cheap really is cheap," I said. "I'd like to, but even then, I'll have to get the money. I hate to ask mom and dad for it."

"I'm sure I know where you can find some in the house," Meri said reluctantly.

"Really?"

"Yes, but don't go getting all weird or I won't tell you where it is."

"Thanks," I said. "Okay, let's go talk to Castor."

Chapter Seven

Castor was waiting patiently outside the shop for us. He was completely oblivious to anything that had gone on inside.

"Well, thanks for coming by," he said.

"I wanted to talk to you about the rent," I said.

"You do?"

"Yes, how much is it per month? What kind of deposit do you need?"

"You're interested in renting it?" he asked.

"I am," I said. "I think this place is perfect for my needs."

He stared at me for a second. Probably waiting for me to tell him I was joking, but I wasn't joking. I really did want to rent the shop as long as it was cheap enough for me to afford.

"So, the ad I've been running says the rent is $500 a month, but I'll go down to $400 if you'll sign a lease today. The deposit is first and last month's rent. You'll need to switch the utilities into your name within seven days and stay current on those," Castor said.

"All right," I said. "I'll need to get the money, but we could meet later."

"Yeah, give me a few hours. I wasn't expecting to do this today. I'll get the lease ready and then we can meet at the diner around six? They're going to have the Reuben on special today, and I wanted to go there for dinner."

The diner.

Great.

"Sure. We can do that," I said. "I can pay the deposit in cash?"

"I always take cash," he said with a smile. "Thank you so much. This is a huge burden lifted off me."

Castor left, and I had to figure out what to do next. I had two huge missions in front of me, and I needed to decide which one was the immediate priority. I had to find out who Merrill's ex-wife was, but I also needed to come up with the cash for the deposit. I didn't have $800 to my name even though I'd just promised to pay that amount to my new landlord. There was also the matter of how I was going to stock the shop after I rented it, but that was a problem for after the lease was signed.

It shouldn't have been, but I never claimed to be the best businessperson. I was winging the whole thing based on intuition.

Given that, I decided to go back to Hangman's House and look for Meri's mystery money. If the house didn't give up the cash, I'd have to ask my parents, and I really, really, really didn't want to do that.

I was crossing the square back to my car when I noticed there was a coffee shop on the opposite side of the square. The Brew Station wasn't the coffee place I remembered in Coventry, but the scent of fresh brewed hit me like a train.

"I need coffee," I said.

"We have coffee at home," Meri answered since not many people were within possible earshot.

"I want that coffee," I said.

"You're supposed to be trying to get money together for a business," Meri said.

"I'll just get one coffee. It's not like I'm going to make it a habit," I said. "Besides, I need the energy. I was almost killed by a ghost minutes ago."

"Whatever, just open up the car on the way by so I can get in. I'm ready for a nap."

"It won't take me long to grab a coffee," I said, but I opened the passenger door for him on the way by.

The Brew Station was a hoot on the inside. It was definitely geared toward tourists with its nearly cartoonish witch theme. It was almost over the top but not quite.

It was a cozy shop, but there was enough room for about a dozen tables. The counter was off to the left, and it sat on top of a display case full of pastries. Those were all witch-themed as well. My favorite were the ghost-shaped sugar cookies. They were covered with a thick layer of white frosting and had two black candy eyes. Underneath and in front of the cash register was a cold drink cooler labeled "potions". It was stocked with artisanal sodas with names like "Hex Berry Cola" and "Under My Spell Strawberry". They were in neat little glass bottles with pictures of witches as the paper labels.

On the back wall behind the counter was a giant, black chalkboard for the menu. The offerings were written in colorful chalk surrounded by drawings of frogs, witch hats, and brooms.

A cheerful-looking woman appeared in the doorway behind the counter. "Welcome to The Brew Station. What can I conjure for you today?"

That was cute.

I didn't study the menu very hard. I just ordered what I wanted and hoped for the best.

"Can I get a hazelnut latte with whole milk, please?"

"You sure can," she said and stepped up to the machines behind the counter. "Do you want whipped cream on that?"

"Always," I said.

"A woman after my own heart."

"I'm Kinsley Skeenbauer. I'm going to be opening a store on the other side of the square in that vacant shop."

"Oooh! The haunted place? That's so cool. I wish that storefront had been available when I was getting ready to open this joint. What kind of shop? Hopefully not a coffee shop," she said with a chuckle, but there was something about her that told me we could be friends even if I was going to open a coffee shop.

"It's going to be a metaphysical gift shop," I said. I thought it sounded better than "witch store".

"Oh, you're going to make a killing," she said completely unironically. Obviously, she didn't know I was the one who found the dead guy the night before. "The tourists are going to eat that up. Making this place witch-themed was the best decision I ever made. You know, I'm surprised no one has opened a metaphysical gift shop yet. I guess maybe a lot of the locals aren't too happy about Coventry's paranormal reputation exploding the way it has. I think it's great. It's certainly good for business."

"I'm excited about the idea," I said.

"Wow, I am so rude. I'm Genevieve Bolton. Everyone calls me Viv." She walked down to the cash register. "You know what, this one's on the house. Congratulations to my new business neighbor," Viv said and handed me the coffee.

"Hey, what do I have to do to get free coffee?" an older man groused from a table behind me.

"Well, Frank, you're probably going to have to steal it from the grocery store," she teased the man.

He just laughed. "You're a pill, Viv."

'That's what keeps you coming back," she said and winked at the old man.

"Thank you so much," I said. "I appreciate the free coffee even if I do think you're just trying to get me hooked."

Viv laughed so hard that her sky blue eyes teared up. She was a middle-aged woman with a curvy figure and long, curly brunette hair. There was just a hint of silver around her temples, and while she wore little makeup, she did have on bright red lipstick.

"We're going to be fast friends," she said. "You have a great day, Kinsley Skeenbauer."

I would have stayed and talked longer because I genuinely liked Viv, but a couple more customers came in. She had work to do, so I took my free coffee and headed out to my car.

Meri looked up at me like I was inconveniencing him as I slid behind the steering wheel. I put the coffee in the cup holder and put the key in the ignition.

"You probably have the last car in the world that doesn't have a push button or remote start," he said as he laid his head back down and closed his eyes.

"I like my car," I said. "It's vintage."

"Suuuuure."

"You still going to show me where that money is?" I asked as I turned the key.

"I guess."

We drove home and I was pleased to find my driveway empty. It wasn't that I didn't love my family, but I wanted to have some space before they all descended on me. I was still adjusting to the fact that coming home was my life, and my entire old life, the one I'd built for myself since I was seventeen, was gone. There was an entire evening of sobbing into a bowl of ice cream while guzzling rum and Coke in my future, but I was still on too much of an adrenaline rush for it to happen yet.

Meri led the way into the house when we got home, and I dutifully followed behind him. I pulled the staircase down for the attic, and we went up.

It was like stepping back in time. A weird tingling sensation ran through my body as I climbed the last step. The books up there practically hummed with potential power.

"Whoa," Meri said. "I don't recall them doing that before."

"So, you feel that too?" I asked.

"Yeah, I guess the attic is happy you're here."

"So, where's this money?" I asked.

I was trying to avoid going to the shelves and picking up one of the books. They were calling to me, but I told myself I had things to do. I knew that if I gave into the books' siren song, I'd be lost up there for days doing research. There would be time enough for that later. I could become the world's most powerful witch or whatever after I had my shi... life together.

It was funny how even then, I still thought those two things were separate.

"There's cash stashed in some of these books," Meri said. "They're like little safes."

"Okay, show me which ones," I said.

Meri walked around the shelves and he occasionally stopped and directed me to a book. I'd take it off the shelf, open it up, and find a stash of bills inside. By the time he said we had all the ones the house was going to give us, I had well over the amount I needed for the deposit.

"This is a lot of money," I said and sat down on one of the chairs to count it.

"Well, you're going to need more than to just pay the rent," Meri said. "You're going to need something to sell there as well. There were a lot of shelves."

"I was going to worry about that later," I said.

"That's the dumbest thing I've heard in like a week," Meri said. He jumped up on the table that sat in front of me and glared at me. "You're signing the lease at dinner tonight. You have to have a plan for the place."

"I want it to be a metaphysical gift shop. It will be a place that tourists can buy stuff but that witches can get supplies too."

"That's actually not a bad idea," Meri said and flicked his tail.

"I thought I was dumb," I said and put the cash down on the table next to him.

"You're slightly less dumb because there's a room full of supplies you can sell in the basement."

"Oh, my goddess, Meri. You're a genius," I said and hugged him.

Chapter Eight

With the rent problem solved and stock to sell at the store after I signed the lease, I still had several hours left before I had to meet Castor. Since I couldn't do anything more for the business until after dinner, I decided to start in on my second problem. I needed to find Merrill's ex-wife.

"How do we find out his ex-wife's name?" I asked.

"I don't know... you could ask somebody," Meri snarked.

"Yeah, but who? I don't want to go back down to the square and just start asking people at random."

"Your parents have lived here for a long time," Meri said. "I know it's a stretch, but they might know."

"I'll call mom," I said.

She answered after two rings. "Hey, sweetie. Are you all right? I heard about what happened at the diner last night."

"I'm fine," I said. "That's actually why I'm calling. I was wondering if you could tell me who Merrill Killian was married to."

"Oh, Kinsley, are you getting involved?" she asked.

"I don't want to, but unfortunately, his ghost has turned into a vengeful spirit with unfinished business. That's what Meri said anyway. He attacked me earlier when I was looking at that vacant shop in the square. Anyway, I'm fine, but the only person he could come up with who might have killed him was his ex-wife. I need to know who she is."

My mother took a deep breath and sighed. "I know I won't talk you out of this, but please be careful. Okay?"

"I will, Mom. Please don't worry."

"All right then. Well, Merrill was married to a woman named Stella Turner. That was her maiden name, and she's gone back to it. She works at the grocery store customer service desk."

"At Mann's?" I asked.

"Yeah, but Mann's isn't what you remember. Bob retired and sold the land and the store name to a company that develops chains. They built a new grocery store on the spot where the old Mann's sat."

"Okay, well at least I'll be able to find it then," I said.

"Call me right away if you need anything," Mom said.

"I promise, I will. I think I'll be all right at the grocery store." I chuckled.

"I know," she said. "But call me if you need anything."

We said our goodbyes, and I went to put my shoes back on.

"I'm coming," Meri said.

"To the grocery store? I doubt they allow cats."

"Get the big tote bag from the hall closet. The one with the blue and magenta flowers. I can ride in there. No one will know."

"Really?"

"Yes, really."

"Fine," I said.

Meri did fit nicely in the tote bag, and I wondered how many times my mother had done the exact same thing. I carried him outside and put him in the passenger side. Soon, we were headed across town to Mann's.

Mom had told me that they'd built a new store, but it was still a bit jarring to see. The small store and gas station had been replaced by a much larger store, and there was no longer a gas station. Instead there was just a large parking lot that wasn't even close to being full.

"I'm going to have to figure out where the gas station is," I said. "There is one, right?"

"There are two," Meri said. "There's one if you go past the diner on your way out of town, and there's another in the newer section of Coventry. It's by all of the new property development on the other side of the square."

"Wow, Coventry really has grown," I said.

"It sort of started to explode a few years back. There are a ton of new houses plus hotels for tourists, but if you just stick to the parts of Coventry you're used to, you wouldn't even know they were there really. They were just sort of Frankensteined onto the edge of town."

I parked in a spot close to the doors and went around to the passenger side to get the Meri bag. The store was as large as one you'd find in the city. The difference being that in a city of any size at all, you'd have several grocery stores to service different areas. As far as I knew, Coventry still only had the one.

We went inside and I stopped at the cooler full of fresh flowers. It just took a brief look around to find the customer service desk located past the cash registers.

There was no one at the desk when we approached. There weren't any customers, and from the looks of it, no one was behind the desk either. We waited a couple of minutes, and a woman finally emerged from the back. She wore a name tag that said "Donna."

"Oh, I'm sorry. I did not know anyone was out here," Donna said. "How can I help you?"

"I'm looking for Stella," I said.

"She is in the dairy section helping with stock. Had a guy call in sick today, and as you can see, I can handle things up here myself," Donna said.

"Thanks."

I left the desk and walked toward the big "Dairy" sign hanging from the ceiling. There I found a woman dressed in jeans and a black t-shirt. She had a burgundy apron tied over her clothes. Her dishwater blonde hair was tied up in a bun at the base of her skull. When she looked up at me, she was vaguely familiar, and then it hit me. She looked just like the woman who'd approached me when I was waiting outside the shop, but it couldn't have been her. I'd just seen that woman an hour or so before, and Stella was working, right? As I looked at her more, I realized she looked very similar, but it wasn't the same woman.

"Can I help you?" Stella asked cheerfully. It sounded genuine, and it was definitely not the same woman.

"Hi.. uh.. my name is Kinsley. There's no easy or good way for me to say this, so I'll just say it. I wanted to talk to you about Merrill," I said and held my breath.

"He's dead," she said matter-of-factly.

"I know. I, uh... found his body at the diner last night. I was hoping you might know who might have killed him," I blurted out.

"Sheriff's already been to talk to me this morning, so who are you?" she said. "You know what, I was about to go on break. As much as I hate to waste that blabbering about Old Merrill, we can go outside. I don't want any of my coworkers hearing anything I've got to say."

I followed her outside to the back of the building where there was an ashtray and a bunch of milk crates set up around it in a circle.

"I hope you don't mind if I smoke because I'm going to," Stella said. She pulled a pack out of her apron followed by a lighter. I stood quietly while she lit the tip and inhaled deeply. "A lot of people hated Merrill. It's hard to say who wanted him dead, and I can't lie. I'm one of those people. There's no point lying about it now, but I was at work last night. I've got two jobs to pay for the mountain of debt Merrill left me in the divorce. I work up at the county hospital on second shift. I was there last night when he died in case you got it in your head that I did it."

"I was just hoping as his ex-wife, you'd know who might have wanted him dead. I didn't think it was you," I lied.

She took another drag of her cigarette and then talked while she exhaled. "You aren't a cop, so who are you?"

"I'm Kinsley Skeenbauer. I'm not a cop, you're right about that. Like I said, I found Merrill last night, and I guess my interest is that I'm sort of a default suspect too. I just moved back to town yesterday, and I guess I'd rather not have everyone thinking I'm a killer right off the bat."

"You're the one my sister was talking about last night. Sorry, I was already on my second whiskey when she came over talking about Merrill being dead and some new chick in town being the number one suspect."

"I think I met her this morning," I said.

"You have to ignore my sister. She doesn't drink or smoke, so her only outlet is her righteous indignation and anger," Stella said and took another deep drag. "Sharlene's husband died a while back, and I can't prove nothing, but I think she took up with Merrill for a while. I wondered where all of her righteousness was then, but then again, I didn't really care either. I mean, other than that, she could do better. Not much better, but better than Merrill. I'm pretty sure she eventually had to break things off with him, but I doubt she ever totally gave up on the idea of rehabilitating him. Once Sharlene gets her teeth in an idea, she's like a pit bull. Never gave up on our good-for-nothing daddy either. Not even when he drank himself into the grave. She'd still tell you to this day, that mean SOB had redeeming qualities. He didn't."

"So are you saying you think your sister might have killed Merrill?"

"Heck, no," Stella said. "Sharlene's nuts but not that kind of nuts. I was just telling you why she was so terrible to you this morning."

"How did you know? I just mentioned meeting her," I said.

"I could tell by the look on your face," Stella said and stubbed out the butt of her cigarette. I was worried she'd have to go back inside, but she pulled out another one and lit it. "As far as who might want Merrill dead, that line forms to the right. I can tell you this, he didn't just run up credit cards. He owed a lot of people money. One in particular had been threatening him for at least a year. Merrill even begged me for help, but I didn't have a cent to give him. I guess I should feel bad about that now, but I have a hard time."

"Who's the man who Merrill owed money to?" I asked.

"I'm not sure I should tell you," she said and took a drag. "I don't care much for Merrill, but I don't want your death on my hands. He's not someone you should be messing around with."

"I can handle myself," I said.

"I can see that about you," she said. "Don't look like you take no stuff from nobody. Okay, I'll tell you, but you have to promise me you won't do anything stupid."

"I won't. I promise I won't get myself into any trouble I can't get back out of."

"All right. His name is Azriel Malum and you'll find him at an abandoned warehouse outside of town. It's an old Coke plant," she said.

"That sounds like a made up name," I said. *Or it's a witch*.

"It most likely is. Azriel is a biker, and that abandoned Coke plant isn't really abandoned. It's their clubhouse."

"A biker?" I said.

"Yep, and not one of those weekend warrior club types either. These are outlaws."

"I didn't know Coventry had an outlaw biker gang," I said and swallowed.

"They rolled in and took over that old Coke plant about four or five years ago. They don't really mess with anyone in town. You have to go looking for trouble with them, but that's exactly what Merrill did. He was mean, but he was dumb too. Welp, I gotta go back in. I can't afford to lose this job, and they get twitchy if our breaks are a minute over our time."

"Thank you," I said.

"Don't thank me yet," she said and started to walk away. "You ain't no killer, so I'd steer clear of Azriel. Let this stuff work itself out."

It was good advice, but I wasn't going to follow it.

Chapter Nine

Again, I still had hours until I needed to meet Castor at the diner. Daytime seemed like a better time to go to an outlaw biker clubhouse, so I got back in the car and looked up the location for the abandoned Coke plant on my phone.

"You're not seriously thinking of going there," Meri said as he climbed over the console to look at my phone.

"It sounds like a good lead," I said. "Why, do you know if this Azriel Malum is a witch or something? The name sounds vaguely demonic too. You think he's a demon?"

"I don't think so, or I'd have probably heard of him. I think what that Stella woman said was correct. He's a biker with an intimidating name."

"And if he's a demon, you can just blow him up," I said.

"We're going, aren't we?" Meri said.

"Yes, right now. I am pulling out of this parking place, and we're going to go ask a biker if he killed someone."

"Sounds like fun," Meri said.

"I knew you'd see it my way."

There were a lot of motorcycles in the dilapidated parking lot of the old Coke plant. It was a bit intimidating considering that Stella had said they were a criminal enterprise, but as long as I wasn't walking into a rogue coven of witches or a nest of demons, I knew I'd be fine. I hoped I could work my magic, anyway.

I located what I thought was the front door based on the loud music coming from inside. As soon as I walked in, everyone stopped and turned to stare at me. Someone turned off the music.

My eyes swept the place for danger. There were several very large men dressed in ripped jeans and leather biker cuts. The inside of the clubhouse was far more opulent than I expected. It was not a dingy, seedy backwater bar.

It was dark inside other than the swirling shapes of black lights that ran up the walls and covered the front of the black wood bar. The tables were the same black wood, but the chair seats were lined with what looked like red velvet. It was all very goth, and again, not what I expected at all.

"A witch and a black cat walk into a bar," a voice boomed from across the room. I squinted my eyes and saw a man sitting in a black throne-type chair against the wall farthest from us. "The punchline, my dear, is that you do not belong here," he said and laughed.

I felt my throat start to close a little, and I swallowed hard. "I'm looking for Azriel Malum," I said as confidently as I could.

It wasn't very confident, though. He knew right away that I was a witch and that meant I wasn't dealing with ordinary men. I'd walked into a bad situation.

"Come here," the man sitting on the throne said.

I went to take a step forward and hesitated. While I wanted to talk to the man, I was concerned about moving away from the door.

"Step forward, woman," he commanded. "You don't need to be afraid. While you're here, you are under my protection. My word is my bond. No harm will come to you."

"Do we believe him?" I asked Meri.

"You're the one that wanted to come here. You knew what you were getting into."

"I don't think I did," I said and swallowed again.

"He said his word is his bond. That's more than a promise. I can get us out of here if he's lying," Meri said.

"Okay."

I walked through the room, and while all of the men stared at me, none of them moved in my direction. As I got closer to the man on the throne, I got a much better look at him. His alabaster skin was like porcelain, and his irises were as black as night. He smiled at me as I drew closer and revealed long fangs.

Vampires.

I'd walked into a vampire den. Of course Stella had no way of knowing, but I should have been more careful. Against one vampire, I would have been fine, but I was surrounded by at least twenty of them.

"Why are you looking for me?" Azriel, the man on the throne, asked.

"Because I've clearly made a mistake," I said.

He laughed. "I like you, witch."

"I'm here because a man was murdered last night. His name was Merrill Killian. His ex-wife told me that he owed you a lot of money. She said you weren't the type of person who it was safe to owe money to, so I came here to talk to you about it. She had no idea who you were, hence I've walked into a vampire den."

"You thought we were just outlaw bikers and that a witch like you could handle herself," he practically purred at me. "Though, you are powerful. I'm not entirely confident we could take you out. Not with your little furry friend there helping you. That's a compliment."

"Thanks, I guess," I said. "So, I think I'll go now. Maybe I'll just let the authorities handle the murder investigation after all."

But then I remembered Thorn. He wasn't a witch, and I didn't want him accidentally walking into this place. The Coke plant was technically in the county, though, so maybe he wouldn't be involved. That meant potentially letting someone else put themselves in harm's way.

"You're not the police, then why are you here? Why would you risk putting yourself in danger to investigate Merrill's death?"

"I just got back to Coventry last night, and I am the one that found the body. That makes me a suspect. It's a long story, but I'm trying to start a business. I just don't want the whole thing further tainted by people thinking I'm a killer. I had some time to burn, so I thought I'd try to clear my name," I said.

"Further tainted?" Azriel raised an eyebrow.

"It's a long story."

"I'm a patient man."

"I'm Kinsley Skeenbauer. My parents are Brighton and Remy Skeenbauer, and my grandmother is Amelda. I'm supposed to be the leader of the Skeenbauer Coven, but I left Coventry when I was seventeen. The whole town, especially the ones who don't know about witches, think I'm just some spoiled brat jerk who ran off and broke my parents' hearts."

"You're Kinsley Skeenbauer?" he said, and I saw something flash in his eyes. Could it have been fear? At the very least it was apprehension.

"I am," I responded.

"Well, Kinsley, I can tell you that I'm disappointed that Merrill is dead. He owed me a lot of money, and I can't get money out of a dead man, now can I?"

"I suppose that's true."

"Hurt him... yes. I would and have done that, but I would not kill someone who still owed me a debt," Azriel said.

"His ex-wife said that he owed a lot of people money. Do you happen to know if he owed money to anyone who isn't as... disciplined as you?"

"I wasn't his nanny," Azriel said shortly. "I only know what he owed me."

"Okay. Thank you," I said and then looked over my shoulder to see if I had a clear path to leave. I did.

"I could help you," he said. The congenial tone had returned to his voice, and I felt myself drawn to him.

He was the spider and I the fly. It would have worked except Meri picked up on it too and protected me. When I felt his hold on me release, I was almost sad for a second. For a split second, the notion that I might enjoy being destroyed by him drifted through my mind.

"But, then I would owe you," I said.

"That's the idea," he said.

"Why would I do that?" I asked. "Why would you even want to help me?"

"The answer to your first question is that I have eyes everywhere. I have my men here, sure, but there are a lot more that owe me. Just because I haven't heard anything about Merrill's death doesn't mean that I don't potentially have access to that kind of information," he said and stood up. His rise from the chair was so fast and fluid that it was almost as if he'd appeared directly in front of me. "As to why I would want to help you, that's simple. Having the most powerful witch I've ever met owe me puts me in a good position." He leaned in and began to whisper in my ear. "I want you close to me."

A shiver ran down my spine, but Meri's magic kept me from being completely intoxicated by his words. "You're dangerous." Was all I could manage to squeak out. I felt my cheeks color with embarrassment at my reaction to him.

"Not to you." His lips were even closer to my ear. "Never to you." Azriel stood back up and gave me some space. I didn't realize until he did that I wasn't breathing. "Nor to anyone close to you."

"I accept your help," I said and then bit my bottom lip hard.

I was an idiot.

"Good," he said and rubbed his hands together before retreating to his throne. "I know where to find you."

And with that, I could tell I was dismissed. I turned to leave, and every vampire in the place stepped back and gave me an even wider berth.

As soon as we were outside and the sun was on my face again, I felt like I was waking from a dream. "I shouldn't have done that," I said as I put Meri into the car. "I can't believe I put myself in debt to a vampire to get information on some stranger's murder."

"Girl, I'm a cat, and a dude, and I probably would have given that man anything he wanted," Meri said. "I tried to help, but even my protection magic can only go so far."

"I've heard you can blow up demons," I said skeptically.

"Yeah, but did you see his eyes?"

"Now I know you're just messing with me," I said.

"Maybe I am. Maybe I'm not," Meri said and curled up on the seat.

I arrived at the diner at ten minutes before six. I wanted to get there and get a table since I figured they'd be busy around that time.

I did have to wait a few minutes to be seated, but just as Reggie was showing me to a booth, I saw Castor pull into a parking spot and make his way into the diner. I waved at him when he came inside.

There was a brown accordion folder tucked under his arm, and I was so eager that I pulled a pen out of my purse and placed it on the table. I left the envelope full of cash out of sight, though.

"Hello, Kinsley," Castor said as he slid into the booth. "I thought for sure you'd stand me up. I can't believe I'm finally going to rent this place out."

"I'm here," I said. "I'm excited to get started on my business."

"Are you sure?" he asked. "I just have to ask one more time. I feel bad about this. Like, if you were my daughter, I'd be ticked off that some old guy was taking advantage of her enthusiasm."

"You're not taking advantage," I said. "I understand the issues with the place, and I'm not worried about it. I've lived in haunted places most of my life. It's like water off a duck's back to me now."

"That's right. You just moved into that Hangman's House, right?"

"Moved back in," I said. "I grew up there."

"That's right. That's right. I heard that. Wow, that place had to be creepy," he said. "It looks like something out of a horror movie."

"It has its quirks," I said. "I don't think I've ever been scared there."

"I didn't mean any offense," Castor said.

"None taken. I think that it's because I grew up there. It just never bothered me. There's a really old cemetery across the street too. It's supposed to be the final resting place of the witches who were hung in the tree out in front of my house. I don't know. It's hard to be afraid when it's been a part of your life for your entire life," I said with a shrug.

"Well, it sounds like I've found my perfect tenant," he said and pulled a small stack of papers out of the folder. "The lease is pretty basic, but I'll give you time to read over it."

While I was reading, the waitress came and took our orders. I got the Reuben with waffle fries just like Castor. It sounded good even though it was not something I would normally order.

I had the lease signed and the money passed over to Castor before our food even arrived. By the time it did arrive, I had just about wound the conversation around to the previous tenant in the shop.

"So, you said something about a bookstore in the shop?" I said as the waitress set the plates down in front of us.

"Yes, it was a bookstore before. That's where all of the shelving came from. The former tenant left in a hurry and never came back for the shelves. If you can't use them, I could have them taken out," Castor offered.

"No, I can use them. They'll be perfect for displaying my stock," I said. "They left in a hurry because of the haunting?"

"That's what the note said."

"They left a note?" I asked. "That's it? That's how they broke their lease?"

"Yep, they up and ran out in the middle of the night. Left a note in the shop that I didn't find until the rent was late. They did the same thing at their townhouse too," Castor said. "Skipped out on the rent and left Coventry."

"I know it's probably none of my business, but who was it?" I asked.

"The tenant or the other landlord?" Castor asked.

"I guess both if you're willing."

"The guy running the bookshop was Lance Bleucastle. The landlord for his townhouse was my friend Jacob Winemaker," Castor said. "Why did you want to know?"

"I guess I'm just curious," I said. "It's strange that he just up and left like that in the middle of the night. Don't you think?"

"Well, I don't know for sure if it was in the middle of the night," Castor said. "Jacob and I didn't know he'd skated out on his leases until the rent came due and he didn't pay. Leaving in the middle of the night is just how people used to do it back in the day."

"Well, thanks for telling me about it," I said.

After that, we ate our food. I didn't want to keep asking him about Lance or the ghost and let our food get cold. It smelled too good to not dive in while the fries were still hot and the sandwich was fresh.

I was about halfway through my sandwich when a woman walked up to the table. "Greta, what are you doing?" Castor asked.

She was glaring at me with a hatred I'd rarely seen. "What are you doing here with her?" Greta said and pointed a finger at me.

I wondered for a moment if the two of them were involved somehow and the woman thought he was cheating on her with me. He wouldn't have been very good at being a philanderer if he brought the woman he was cheating with to the diner, though.

"We're here signing papers," I said before Castor could say anything. "I'm leasing the shop in the square."

"Shut up!" she hissed at me.

"Greta, there's no reason for you to act that way," Castor said and stood up. "No reason at all."

"You know she's a killer, right? She's a killer and you leased your shop to her?" Greta's voice was rising to a crescendo. "Not only that, but she's from that Skeenbauer family. She's one of those freaks that turned this town into Satan's playground!"

"Satan's playground?" Castor asked with an amused chuckle. "You don't even go to church, Greta. Why are you in here hollering about Satan's playground?"

By that time, the entire diner had turned to look at us. Reggie had just delivered a large order to a table across the dining room, and she was scooting over in our direction as fast as possible. Reggie made it about halfway over when the one guy in the whole restaurant who wasn't paying attention to what was going on around him scooted his chair back and tripped her. She fell down and managed to catch herself with her hands before her face hit the floor, but she dropped her tray. It clattered loudly, and no one made a move to help her.

I started to get up to go to her, but Greta must have thought I was getting up to fight or something.

She grabbed my Coke glass and threw what was left in it in my face.

"Greta, that's enough," Castor said. "No, you've left me no choice." He pulled out his phone and dialed 911.

I dodged Greta throwing the glass at me and rushed over to Reggie. After I helped her to her feet, I looked around to see that Greta was marching over to us.

"Take her in the back," Castor said to Reggie.

"Come on," Reggie said and grabbed my wrist.

She pulled me through the dining room and behind the counter. We went through a black swinging door that led into the kitchen and prep area.

"Is she going to follow us back here?" I asked.

But just then, the cook came around from the grill area and went back through the door. Before it stopped swinging, I could see that he'd put himself between Greta and us.

"Nah, he's got it," Reggie said. "He won't let her back here."

"That's the second time today that some woman has gotten in my face and called me a killer. That and insulted my family."

One of Reggie's knees was an angry red color and skinned. It must have been the one that hit the floor first. Without thinking, I waved my hand over it and healed the wound.

Reggie must have felt something because she stretched her leg out and looked at it. "Huh, I thought I skinned my knee pretty bad when I went down on it," she said.

"Looks like you're bouncier than you thought," I said.

"Are you calling me fat?" she asked and then laughed.

"Oh, yeah, you've got horribly fat knees," I said.

She cracked up at that, and it made me feel a little better too. A couple of minutes later, the cook came back through the door.

"Crazy pants gave up and left," he said. "But you guys better stay back here until Thorn gets here just in case."

Chapter Ten

Thorn arrived pretty quickly. There were a lot of witnesses that told him Greta attacked me. He wanted to get out there and arrest her, but he pulled me aside first.

"Can you come outside and talk with me for a quick second?" he asked.

"I need to be going anyway," Castor said with his wrapped up half sandwich and fries in a white paper bag. "Call me if you need anything."

"What was that about with Castor?" Thorn asked when we got outside. "Why would you need anything from him?"

"That's why I was here at dinner with him," I said. "I rented his shop space down at the town square."

"You're going to open a shop in the square now?" Thorn sounded incredulous. "After what just happened here?"

"One, I'd already signed the lease and handed over the deposit when Greta attacked," I said and took a deep breath. "And two, I already told you I wanted to open a shop. I said it this morning."

"I thought I said that it would be better for you to wait until you're not a murder suspect anymore," Thorn said.

"You did, but I don't take my marching orders from you."

"You're impossible," he said.

"Are you mad at me?" I asked, but it was my turn to be incredulous. "How can you be mad at me? You don't even know me," I said and put my hands on my hips.

"You're right. I don't," he said and threw up his hands. "Sorry I tried to help. I'm going to go find Greta and arrest her for assaulting you."

He turned to leave without saying another word, and I instantly felt terrible. We'd clicked almost immediately, and I could tell by the way Thorn was acting that he'd felt it too. I'd been a total jerk pretending like it never happened.

"Thorn, wait," I called after him.

"I've got a job to do right now. I'll talk to you later."

"Great," I said as he got into his car.

"You two are going to get married." Reggie's voice from behind me made me jump six inches off the ground.

"What?" I asked.

"You and Thorn are going to get married," she said.

"I heard you," I said. "What I don't understand is what the heck you are talking about."

"Sparks like that flying between two people who just met? Mhm. I give it a year."

"There were no sparks. He's just gotten himself all wound up over... I don't know actually."

"What he's wound up over is you. I've never seen Thorn even look in another woman's direction more than once."

"He was mad at me for not listening to him," I said.

"Yeah, and he's got no reason to be, right? He's overprotective of you out of nowhere? I read enough romance novels to know that means there is a wedding in the not so distant future."

"Romance novels aren't realistic," I said.

"Nothing in Coventry is."

"He's just being weird," I countered.

"Uh huh," Reggie said and winked at me. "So, what are you up to now?"

"I really should work on getting my business up and running, but there's something I need to take care of first," I said.

"What's that?"

"I need to figure out who killed Merrill," I said.

"Ooooh. No wonder Thorn was mad at you."

"That wasn't why, but it doesn't matter. I want to open a business, and I need to prove I didn't kill the guy. Otherwise, these people are going to keep showing up and screaming at me about how I'm a killer from a weird family. It will ruin my business."

"How are you going to do that?" Reggie asked.

"I can't tell you. It's a secret."

"Ooooh, a secret? Now you have to tell me."

"Seriously, I can't. I can't tell anybody what I'm about to do."

"Then I'll just follow you," she said.

"What?" I couldn't believe what I was hearing.

"You heard me. Either you drag my bored behind along with whatever shenanigans you're about to get into, or I'll just follow you," she said completely seriously.

"Reggie... don't you need to get back to work?"

"Nah, I worked closing last night. The dinner rush is over and a bunch of people left because of Greta. The other waitress is going to handle the floor for the night. It was mostly her tables that cut and run," she said with a chuckle. "So, where are we going?"

She was completely serious about following me, so for a moment, I considered going home. It would have been easier if I'd just gone home and let

Reggie follow me there, but I felt like I had to go to Merrill's place.

"Fine, you can go, but I have to stop by my house and get my cat first," I said.

"Why?" she asked, her brow all scrunched up.

"Because what we're about to do isn't technically legal, and he's my emotional support animal," I said.

"This sounds intriguing," she said and rubbed her hands together. "Wait, you bring your emotional support cat with you when you break the law?"

"Yes," I said simply. "So, are you still coming?"

What I didn't tell her was that I was bringing Meri for protection. I couldn't wipe her memory if she got spooked and decided to call the sheriff, but Meri probably could. He could do it to protect me. I hoped.

Reggie got in my car and was quiet while I was pulling out of the diner parking lot. It wasn't until we were out on the street and headed for Hangman's House that she finally said something.

"I overheard something earlier today that I thought might be of interest," she said. "That's why I wanted to come along. I watch a lot of those true crime shows, and I just have to know what happened here."

"What did you hear?" I asked.

"Well, I was serving these two guys lunch, and I heard one of them say Merrill's name. He said it all quiet like he thought I was too far away to hear, but I have good ears."

"The guy said his name, but what else did he say?" I asked.

"Well, he said that Merrill owed him money for some house repairs. A lot of money apparently. He said that now that Merrill was good and dead, he was going to file a lien against his estate. He was getting his money out of him one way or another."

"That sounds interesting," I said. "Do you know who he was?"

"Yeah, his name is Jerry Sprigs. He's one of the only contractors in town that's not working on building new houses over in the new subdivisions. So he's just about the only guy available for remodels or repairs. Well, he was available. I'm pretty sure he's all booked up now too."

"Hey, do you know where Merrill lived? I can look it up if you don't."

"I do," Reggie said. "He lives down the street from where I grew up."

"Well, after we get my cat, I'll let you tell me how to get there then," I said.

We pulled up in front of Merrill's house less than twenty minutes later. He lived in a section of

Coventry I hadn't spent much time in. The houses were smaller than the grand old Victorians most of the witches lived in.

Instead, Reggie's and Merrill's old neighborhood was filled with post-WWII houses. Some of them were what I'd heard affectionately referred to as "Cracker Jack boxes."

There was police tape tied to one side of the front porch, but it was flapping in the wind. "We're going to get in big trouble if we go in there and it's a crime scene," Reggie said.

"Look at the tape blocking the door, it's ripped and blowing in the wind. That means it's not secure anymore," I said as we got out of the car.

"Hey, we should pull around to the alley," Reggie said. "Get back in."

I did, and I was about to ask what got into her, but I saw it. One of Merrill's neighbors was peeking out her curtain at us. I don't know how I'd been so stupid to just park right in front of the house.

We drove the car around to the alley and parked it there. Well, not right behind his house. I parked it a block away, and we hurried down the alley to his house.

Merrill's back yard was surrounded by chain-link fence, but his gate wasn't locked. We went through it and hurried through the yard.

The house didn't have a door in the back. Instead it was around the side of the house off the driveway. We were right in sight of the neighbor's window, so I used a little magic to unlock the door.

"Oh, good. It's unlocked," I said as we went inside.

"You would have thought the sheriff's office would have made sure it was locked," Reggie said.

"Yeah, you would have thought so. Maybe there's something wrong with the lock," I offered.

"Could be," Reggie said as she looked around. "You sure you want to do this?"

I could understand why she was asking. Merrill's place was a disaster. "This is horrible," I said. "You don't think they did this when they were searching, do you?"

"No, this is the kind of mess he had to work on for years to accomplish," Reggie said. "Maybe we shouldn't be in here. This house could be a biohazard zone or something."

"I'm sure we'll be fine," I said, but I hurried out of the kitchen and into the living room. "Please do a protection spell," I whispered into the bag Meri was riding in. "This place is probably a biohazard."

"What was that?" Reggie asked as she walked into the living room. "Were you talking to the cat?"

"Yeah, I mean, he is my emotional support cat. I don't like this mess at all. You're right, though. We should take a look around and see what we can find fast. Then, let's get out of here. It stinks."

Fortunately, the house was small. But I doubted that Thorn and his deputies had been able to find anything in the house. There were beer cans and old papers and magazines everywhere. Each room, including the bathroom, had its very own stack of dirty dishes too. I'd never seen anything like it.

We looked around for a good ten minutes, and all we found was trash. One thing I learned was that apparently Merrill hadn't been killed in the house and dropped off at the diner because there was no real crime scene in the house.

Merrill's bedroom had a twin bed and a desk set up in one corner. I was heading over to the desk to see if there was anything but dirty dishes and empty beer cans on it when Reggie called out to me. "Your boyfriend is here! The neighbors must have called the cops. We gotta go."

Right as I was turning to run from the room, I saw an invoice on the desk from Reliable Construction. I grabbed it quickly and then sprinted from the room.

We lucked out that Thorn went to the front door first. He must have had a key, but as he was coming in the front door, Reggie and I were running out the back.

Chapter Eleven

We made it out the back gate before Thorn appeared in the yard. "Hey!" he yelled at us, and I shoved the invoice into my bag.

"Oh, hi, Thorn!" Reggie called back cheerfully.

"What are you two doing?" he asked as he closed the distance between us.

"We were going to break in and have a look around," Reggie said, and I shot her a death stare. What was she doing? "I mean, it was my idea. I think Kinsley just came along to talk me out of it, and she finally did. Thank goodness or you'd probably have to arrest us right now."

"The neighbors called it in and said they saw two women going in the back door" Thorn said and crossed his arms over his chest.

"We went into the yard, but we change our minds. So, we came back out here and we were just leaving" Reggie said.

I held my breath and prayed that Thorn didn't ask me to confirm her story. While I was impressed with her ability to spin a yarn to the sheriff, I didn't want to lie to him. I didn't know if I could lie to him.

Thorn's piercing eyes fell on me and he watched me for a second. Just then, Meri popped his head out of the top of the bag.

"Do you have Meri with you?" Thorn asked with a chuckle.

"I do" I said and felt my cheeks turn bright red.

"Well, I guess I don't believe that you'd break into a house with your cat in a tote bag. That's a little too absurd for even this town."

Oh, if he only knew.

"See, so can we go?" Reggie asked hopefully.

"Yeah, you guys can go, but Reggie, please don't drag our newest resident into any more situations where I have to be involved" he said and started to leave. "Oh, and if I catch you breaking into any more houses, I will arrest you both. And the cat."

"I'm sorry" I said, but before Thorn could respond, Reggie grabbed my hand and yanked me down the alley.

"Come on, let's move" she said as she pulled me toward the car. "He said we could go, so let's get out of here before he changes his mind."

"He knew" I said as I got into the car.

"Yeah, he totally did, but either he couldn't prove it or he didn't want to arrest you" Reggie said. "Either way, when he checks the place out, he'll see we didn't do anything."

"Well, I did find an invoice from Reliable Construction on the desk in Merrill's bedroom and I took it" I said.

"Oh, yeah? That's Jerry's company."

"That house didn't look like it had any kind of remodeling done" I said.

"Where's the invoice?" Reggie asked.

"In the bag with Meri."

She dug it out and looked it over. "It doesn't look like there was any remodeling because it was foundation work. This unpaid invoice is for a lot of money too, and he just got it a couple of weeks before he died. I doubt he paid it."

"How much?" I asked.

"Twelve grand."

"That is a lot of money. I wonder if it was enough for this Jerry guy to kill over, though?"

I was about to ask Reggie where she wanted to go when she got a text. "Hey, we'll have to figure that out later. Can you take me back to the diner so I can get my car? My mother's in Shady Acres and they need me to come check on her."

"Is she okay?" I asked.

"Probably. It's usually nothing serious. There's a nurse that works there my mom doesn't like and sometimes they get into it."

"Sure, I'll drop you off. You can call me if you need anything."

I dropped her off and headed back to my house where I found Thorn's cruiser waiting in my driveway. The driveway was double wide, so I pulled in without blocking him. As I got out of my car, he got out of his.

"Fancy meeting you here" I said and then instantly felt really, really stupid. "Sorry. That was dumb. I'm just..."

"Can we talk inside?" His tone was serious.

"Sure. Yeah. Come in" I said and walked up to the front door. "Can I get you a coffee or a Coke?" I asked once we were inside. "Come on in and sit down."

"I'll take a beer if you have it" he said.

"Really?"

"Yeah, I'm off duty. It's fine if you don't have one. I don't want to impose."

"No, of course. You're not imposing. Let me grab one from the fridge."

I had no idea if I even had any beer, but I was about to find out how much the house liked Thorn. I walked into the kitchen and grabbed the refrigerator handle. When I opened it, there was a six-pack on the top shelf. "Do you like Wicked Dark Ale?" I called out into the living room.

"It's one of my favorites," he called back.

Apparently, the house liked him a lot. "Okay. I'll be right there."

I grabbed his beer and myself a Coke and walked back out into the living room. Thorn was seated in one of the wingback chairs, so I set his beer in front of him and plopped down on the sofa.

"Is this a social call, or is what you need to talk to me about so serious you need a drink?" I asked.

He studied me again, and again, it felt like his gaze went right through me. I felt exposed around Thorn in a way I never had around another man, but I also felt safe. It was like he could see right into me, but I knew he'd never use that against me.

"I heard you went out to the old Coke plant" he said gravely.

"How would you have heard that?" I asked too quickly.

"Ah, answering a question with a question. That's classic deflection" Thorn said just before taking a long draw from his beer. "I'd hoped I was wrong."

"I mean... how would you even know that?"

"Kinsley, if you don't think I have eyes in that clubhouse, then you have vastly underestimated me" he said.

"So what? You have a vampire informant?" I asked.

"Given what this town is and what you are, is that really so outlandish?" he asked.

"So, now you're answering a question with a question" I said.

"You got me there" he said and leaned forward. "My informant told me that you now owe Azriel Malum a favor."

I had to wonder if his informant had also told him what kind of effect Azriel had had on me. I suddenly felt as though I'd done something wrong. I didn't want Thorn to know how attracted I'd been to Azriel. It was really bizarre. Why did I care?

"He's going to look into Merrill's death. We could solve the murder with that information." I was getting defensive.

"We?" Thorn said with an incredulous laugh. "I'm the sheriff. You shouldn't be making promises to the likes of Azriel Malum just so I don't have to do my job." Thorn shook his head. "I'm taking the favor on. Whatever he ends up asking you for, I'll fulfill it."

That actually made me laugh. "I don't think you're going to be able to fulfill Azriel."

"What?" he said and scooted to the edge of his chair. "So you knew what he might want, and you agreed anyway? Why? Why would you do that, Kinsley?"

The way he said my name burned me with shame. I'd been under some sort of spell when I was near Azriel, but away from him as I dealt with the hurt in Thorn's eyes, I wasn't under any kind of spell.

"It's because I'm a witch" I said and hoped that could save the conversation. "Whatever else you're thinking is from some sort of misplaced jealousy."

"Misplaced jealousy?" Thorn's cheeks turned red, and I knew I'd embarrassed him. "I just met you. What I care about is your mother and father. They are my friends, and I'd hate to see their hearts broken again because you got yourself caught up with an evil vampire."

"My parents?" I said and stood up. "Look, I was seventeen years old when I left this town, but I am a grown woman now. I don't need your approval or theirs. I certainly don't need you going all alpha on me and pretending like you can defend my honor with Azriel. I don't need my honor defended."

"Fine" Thorn said and stood up. "Fine." He started for the door.

"Wait, where are you going?" I said. "You haven't finished your beer." For some reason, I didn't want him to leave that way.

"What?" He stopped and turned around.

"You haven't finished your beer" I said.

"You want me to stay?" His eyes narrowed and his brow knitted.

"I don't want you to go" I said. "Not like this."

He walked back over to the chair and sat down. "I understand why you left" he said. "I loved my old man to pieces, but there were times I wanted to run too."

"It was never about my family" I said. "I never wanted to get away from my family. I just didn't want to be what I am."

"The head of your coven?" he asked.

"Yeah, that. I wanted a regular life. Plus there's all this stuff in the prophesy about me saving everyone. That's a heavy burden. I guess in my dumb young head, I thought that if I left, it would never happen. Or maybe that fate would pick someone else."

"That's not the way it works" Thorn said.

"How would you know?" I teased, and he smiled. "Anyway, at this point, I think all of that saving the world stuff is metaphorical."

"Probably. A lot of that ancient prophesy type stuff usually is."

"Would you like another beer?" I asked when I noticed he'd nearly drained the first since he'd sat down.

"I shouldn't" he said.

"Why, because you're leaving right away?" I asked.

"No" he said. "Not unless you want me to."

"Let me get you another beer" I said. "Maybe I'll have a glass of the Moscato I have in the fridge."

There was an awkward silence that hung in the air when I came back. After I handed Thorn his beer, we both sat and sipped our drinks without saying anything for a few minutes. Finally, I couldn't stand it anymore, and I blurted out a question that had been bothering me since Reggie had put ideas in my head earlier.

"So, what's going on here?"

"What do you mean?" Thorn asked.

I let out a sigh. "I mean this" I said and waved my hand through the air indicating him and our drinks on the table. "We've been sniping at each other like we know each other since right after we met. You're frustrated with me like you know me. Is it really just because you're friends with my parents?"

I grabbed my wine and took a huge gulp of the sweet, fruity nectar.

"Well, that's strange" Thorn said as he looked at me with fascination.

"What? What is it?"

"The teal parts of your hair are turning pink" he said. "With the purple, it's more unicorn than mermaid now."

I'd almost forgotten that my hair changed colors with my powers or my mood. Or whatever.

"You're deflecting by talking about my hair" I said and took another gulp of my wine. "But, that's fine. If you don't want to talk about it, or if I'm nuts and there's nothing to talk about."

"I've wanted to ask you out," he said and took an equally large gulp of his beer. "Actually, I've wanted to kiss you since the moment I laid eyes on you the first time." Thorn's eyes went wide. "Crud. I did not mean to say that out loud."

"You know you could," I said.

"Kiss you?"

"Ask me out on a date," I said, but I'd meant the other too.

"Would you like to have dinner with me, Kinsley?"

"When?"

"Are you available tomorrow night?"

"I'll need to check my calendar," I said and his shoulders slumped. "I'm teasing. Yes, I'll have dinner with you tomorrow night. What time?"

"I'll pick you up after my shift. I'll need to go home and shower first, but I can be here by six if that will work."

"Sure," I said.

Before either one of could say anything else, Thorn's cell phone rang.

"I have to take this," he said and stood up.

"Go ahead."

He walked into the dining room and answered. I didn't hear much of the conversation except for him saying that he understood and that he'd be right there. When he came back out, his face fell.

"Crap," he said.

"What? What's wrong?"

"There was a bad accident out on the highway. The state police have asked for my help. I said I'd go, but I've had two beers. I feel fine, but I shouldn't. I'll have to call them back and see if one of my deputies can go."

"No. I can help you with that," I said.

"With the beers?" He seemed puzzled.

"Yeah, come here," I said. "I can sober you right up."

He crossed the room and I stood up so that we were standing face to face. I took both of Thorn's hands in mine and closed my eyes. My mind's eye searched inside of him until I found what I was looking for, and then I did a little chant that I remembered from when I was much younger. When I opened my eyes, Thorn was looking down at me, but that time, I didn't shrink from his gaze.

"What did you do?" he asked and squeezed my hands tighter.

I giggled suddenly feeling a bit tipsier than I had when I started. "It was some empathy magic. I took any intoxication of yours into me. You're a big guy, so I've got a good buzz going on now."

His lips drew back into a grimace.

"What's wrong?" I asked.

"I have this overwhelming urge to kiss you," he growled. "But, I can't because you're drunk."

"I'm not drunk," I protested.

He kissed my forehead and then my cheek. "I have to go."

When Thorn let go of my hands, I felt an empty spot inside of me. That was the first time I really knew I was in trouble.

Chapter Twelve

A couple of hours after Thorn left, I was completely sober, and it was still fairly early. Instead of just finding a movie to watch or maybe playing a video game on my laptop, I decided to go talk to Jerry Sprigs.

I looked him up on Google and found his home address. My phone gave me the option to get directions, and since the older-than-dirt GPS in my car didn't work, I accepted.

"Where are you going?" Meri asked as he sauntered into the living room from the dining room.

"I'm going to go over to this Jerry Sprigs's house and ask him about his connection to Merrill," I said.

"Can't you just read a book or something?" Meri asked.

"No. I want to start moving inventory to the shop tomorrow, and I need this cleared up."

"You know this guy is going to think you're a real loony-toon showing up on his doorstep to ask him about a murder," Meri said. "You might even tick him off if he gets the impression you're accusing him."

"The whole town already thinks I'm terrible and possibly a killer. I'll take my chances," I said.

"I'm going," Meri said.

"Great, now the whole town will think I'm the crazy cat lady too," I said.

"You're welcome," Meri snarked.

We got in the car, and I set my phone down on the seat. Much to my surprise, Meri could actually read the directions and help me navigate. That was good because I hated the little voice when you had the turn-by-turn directions on. All those years and they never got a better voice. The female robot voice was so creepy.

Since I wasn't breaking in, I pulled my car up to the curb in front of Jerry's house. I tried to get Meri to stay in the car, but he insisted on coming in. Knowing I was never going to talk him out of it, I opened the passenger door for him and we made our way up the walk to Jerry Sprigs's small front porch.

I heard what I thought could have been shouting coming from inside the house somewhere. It also could have been a television turned up loud, so I rang the bell. The noise inside stopped, but I still didn't know if I'd interrupted an argument or someone inside had just turned the TV down when they heard the doorbell.

Eventually, the door opened. A man in his late thirties with shaggy brown hair and a mustache stood there sizing me up. "Can I help you?" he finally said.

Seconds later, a woman appeared behind him. Instantly, I recognized her as the woman who'd confronted me in front of the shop. Fury overcame her face, and she tried to push past her husband.

"Jerry, let me through," she barked at him.

"Whoa, woman. What is your deal?" he asked without moving.

"Get out of my way," she demanded.

"You need to chill. You stay in this house, you hear me," he demanded.

Somehow, he managed to step out onto the front porch and close the front door without her getting by. I was certain that his actions were only going to enrage her more, but she did listen to him and stay in the house.

I waited for the television to come back on, but it didn't. So, either I'd interrupted an argument, or she was watching us from one of the house's windows.

"Why does my wife want to attack you?" he asked.

"I don't know," I said. "I saw her in the town square this morning. I was waiting to see about a rental space. She came across the street and started yelling at me about my family basically being trash. She also thinks I killed Merrill Killian."

"I don't know about the family thing, but I know she doesn't really think you killed Merrill," he said and rubbed the back of his neck. "You're Kinsley Skeenbauer, right?"

"I am," I said.

"So, if she did that earlier today, what are you doing here now?" Jerry asked.

"I didn't know she was here or your wife. I came here to talk to you."

"Me?"

"Yeah, my friend works at the diner, and she overheard you telling someone that you were going to put a lien on Merrill's estate because he owed you a lot of money," I said.

"Why do you care?" Jerry asked. "Did he owe you money too?"

"No, I care because your wife isn't the only person who thinks I killed him," I said. "I'm trying to start a business here in Coventry, and I don't need this hanging over my head."

"So, you're here to find out if I killed him?" Jerry asked.

I could tell by the sudden shift in his demeanor that he was offended. I had to think fast, or he was probably going to open his front door and let his wife have a go at me.

"No, of course I don't think it's you," I said as sincerely as possible. "I just heard what you said about the lien, and I wondered if you knew anyone else who might have had the same interests. Like someone who he owed more money to or someone that might not have handled it as professionally as you are." Complementing him did the trick, and I saw Jerry physically relax. "I know he owed some biker loan shark money."

"Yeah, I've already looked into that. It went nowhere," I said.

"Wow, you're on top of this," Jerry said and took a step closer to me. "It's admirable to see such a beautiful woman have such a take-charge attitude."

Gross.

I took a step back and almost fell off the small concrete porch, but Meri's magic caught me before I could fall on my butt in the grass. I decided to use Jerry's sudden shift in... attitude... toward me to my advantage.

"So, where were you the night he died?" I asked in a fake flirtatious voice. "I mean, just so I can cross you off my list." I winked at him, but I also almost threw up a little. Oh, well, a girl had to do what a girl had to do.

"I worked until nearly eleven at Mary Water's house over on Crow's Mill Street," he said and put his hands up in mock surrender. "Am I off the hook now, officer?" He winked back at me.

I had to stifle a repulsed shiver that ran down my spine. I needed to get out of there before the guy either tried to grope me or his wife busted down the front door and ripped my hair out.

"I swear I wasn't here to accuse you," I said and turned just enough so that I could back down the steps to the sidewalk without falling. "Well, it's getting late. I've got to run."

"Hey, I thought we had something here," he protested.

"Your wife is right inside," I said and hurried away.

As I was getting in the car, Jerry was looking back and forth between me and his house. It was like he was trying to figure out if he should come after me or just go inside. I got out of there fast and didn't look back.

Chapter Thirteen

I decided that I'd had enough run-ins with weirdos, vampires, and freaks that day, so I went home to watch a movie and go to bed. I was in my pajamas on the couch with a bowl of popcorn and my laptop when I got a text message.

Sorry I had to leave in such a hurry. I'm home now. I hope you have a good night. The text was from Thorn.

It's okay. You can make it up to me tomorrow. I'm glad you made it home all right and didn't have to be out on the highway all night. I texted back.

I was just there to make sure the wreck didn't cause a pile-up. Traffic reduced significantly after I arrived, so I didn't have to stay long.

That's great. I'm looking forward to tomorrow. I answered, hoping that didn't sound too desperate.

Not as much as I am. ;-) It's been a long day, but I'm glad we got to have a drink together.

It was nice. I'll let you sleep, and we'll talk tomorrow. Good night, Thorn. I said.

Good night, Kinsley.

I set my phone down and restarted my movie. After a few minutes, my face started to hurt from smiling.

Fortunately, a sinister tapping on the glass at my front window saved me from my happiness. "What is that?" Meri asked. He'd been snoozing next to me and the sound startled him awake.

"Someone's tapping on the glass," I said. "Why wouldn't they knock on the door?"

"My guess is that it's not a normal visitor," Meri said.

"Should we just ignore it?" I asked.

"Probably."

"That's it? Probably?"

"Yeah, I mean, what do you want?" Meri asked.

The sound changed from a tapping to a thud like the palm of a hand thumping against the glass. "I'm going to go have a look," I said.

I went over to the window with Meri right on my heels. I pulled back the curtain to find Merrill's ghost standing on the other side.

"He can't come in because of the protection spells around the house," Meri said.

"Should I go talk to him? Maybe he remembers something," I said hopefully.

"No, you should not go out there," Meri said. "If he's back, he must have gotten the energy from somewhere. I'd put my money on rage."

"You don't think I should at least try? I can probably take on one ghost. He only got me last time because he caught me off guard."

"It isn't worth the risk. I'm sure he doesn't remember the day he died," Meri said.

"I'll just open the window, then," I said. "If he can't come in the house, then he can't come in the window, right?"

"Maybe put a line of salt across it just in case," Meri said. "And I'll cast a circle around us. Nothing formal."

"Okay."

I went to the kitchen and got the container of salt from the pantry. After I spread a thick line of salt over the window sill, I opened it a few inches.

"What is it, Merrill?" I asked.

"I remembered something," he said.

"About who killed you?" I asked hopefully.

"No, not that late in the day. I remember something from that morning. I had to meet with someone."

"Do you remember who?" I asked.

"No, but it was a woman. A woman with black hair and blue eyes. I can see her, but I can't remember her name. I think it was on the first floor."

"Okay," I said.

"And you better figure out who killed me." That came out as a snarl. "Or I'll make you wish you were never born."

"That's about enough of that," I said and closed the window.

I shut the curtain and the thumping on the glass started again. Knowing he could only be annoying and not actually come into the house, I went back over to the sofa and put my headphones on. I turned the movie up loud enough that I couldn't hear him knocking on the window anymore. Meri shot me a disgruntled look and darted into the hole in the wall that led into his tunnels.

The next morning I got up and decided it was time to start taking stuff from the basement over to the shop. First, I had to deal with the stuff in the trailer so I could use it to move stock. I was lucky that I had the rental for a few more days and wouldn't have to pay more.

I hooked the car back up to the trailer and maneuvered it so the trailer was backed up nearly to the porch. Since no one was around, I used a little magic to make the lifting a little easier. Unfortunately, that was using my magic for personal gain and I ended up with three gnarly paper cuts from the edges of cardboard boxes and I hit my elbow hard on the side of the truck. I didn't dare heal the minor injuries, though, when I realized it was my penalty for using the magic for personal gain.

I did not use magic to help me load the truck. I didn't want to cut any more of my fingers or end up dropping something heavy on my foot. By the time I had everything loaded, I was already tired and more than ready for second breakfast.

When I'd been in the Brew Station before, I remembered that she'd had pastries and there were hot breakfast sandwiches on the menu as well. That sounded better than cooking something for myself, so I drove the trailer down to the square and backed it into a parking place. After I unhitched it, I parked the car next to it and headed over to the coffee house.

It was fairly early, but there was already a tour walking through the square. As I walked into the Brew Station, the scent of fresh roasted coffee beans, bacon, and biscuits filled my nose. My mouth began to water and my stomach growled.

"Hey, Viv," I said when it was my turn at the counter. "Do you bake fresh biscuits back there?"

"Oh, no. I get them fresh every day from the bakery over on West Vine. It's called the Lovin' Oven. It's witch-themed too now, but I'm not so sure about that. Makes me think of baking kids like that fairy tale, but anyway, the woman who owns it is Carla Sparks. She's great, and she makes the best biscuits. She's from the South. Anyway, I use them to put together the breakfast sandwiches on the menu. The tots on the menu are just regular tater tots like from the store, but the oil's always fresh and I use that flaky pink Himalayan salt in them. Makes them extra special," she said with a wink. "Would you like to try a sandwich?"

"I would," I said. "I'd like the sausage biscuit with a large tots."

"And a hazelnut latte?" Viv offered.

"Yes, please. Extra-large."

"Double espresso?" she tempted, and I knew I shouldn't, but I couldn't turn it down.

"Yes, thank you."

I left the order area and walked over to the cash register to check out. When Viv was done, she brought my sandwich and tots over in a white paper bag and my latte in a to-go container. She must have seen me looking at them because she said something.

"I'm sorry if I was too presumptuous. I saw you pull that trailer up to your new shop, and I figured you were ready to work."

"It's okay. I'm just glad you're not hinting that I'm not welcome," I said and pulled the cash for my order out of my wallet.

"Never," she said with a smile. "I can get you a tray for your food and a mug for the coffee if you want to stay."

I was about to say that I would stay but the bag and to-go cup were fine, but I saw Meri sitting outside the shop staring in at me. "You know what, I should get over there and get working, but can I trouble you for an extra side of bacon before I go?" I said.

"Not a problem," Viv said with a smile. "He's a biggun." She saw Meri looking too.

"He is, and he loves his bacon," I said. "Of course, I never give him too much."

"Never," Viv said conspiratorially. "That will be two dollars, and I'll just wrap it up in a piece of parchment for you."

"Thank you."

"Hey, and if he wants to come in in the afternoon sometime, I'm sure my regulars won't mind. Sorry, I can't have him in here during the morning rush."

"Oh, thank you," I said. "Maybe we will come visit some afternoon."

I put the bacon in my bag and headed out the door. Meri gave me a look when I exited the coffee shop, but there was a gaggle of tourists headed for the Brew Station, so he stayed quiet until we were across the street.

"I didn't get a key," I said. "In the middle of the fray when I signed the lease, I didn't get the key."

"You also left me at home this morning," Meri said.

"You were sleeping."

"I wasn't that asleep," Meri scoffed.

"Could have fooled me," I said. "So, do I just use a little magic to go in and make up an excuse about the place being unlocked, or do I call Castor and wait outside?"

"I don't care," Meri said.

"Sorry, Meri. I did get you bacon."

"I guess call him and we'll wait. It's nice out this morning. We could eat in the car or over on one of the benches in the square."

"You're right. We'll eat on a bench. We can tourist watch," I said.

Unfortunately, we finished our breakfast and we still had fifty minutes left before Castor was supposed to arrive with the key. I decided that even though it wouldn't go anywhere, we'd go into the courthouse and look for the woman Merrill's ghost had mentioned the night before. Meri couldn't really go in the courthouse with me, so he sauntered over to the trailer. He lay on top of it so he could watch people and bask in the sun.

Inside the courthouse was a cavernous open area with elevators directly across from the entry doors. Off to each side were doors that led into offices and hallways that took you deeper into the building. There was also a set of stairs on each side.

To my left was a small marble counter with a woman seated behind it. There was a sign on the front that said "information". The woman was older with a gray beehive hairdo perched atop her head. Her thin lips were coated in a layer of blood-red lipstick, and a pair of cat-eye glasses sat perched at the end of her nose.

"Hello," I said as I approached.

"The copier is twenty-five cents per page," she said.

"What?"

"It's twenty-five cents per page for the copier. You pay me for how many pages you need, and I'll give you a code. Photocopying is no longer free."

"Oh, okay," I said. "I'm not here for the copier. I'm looking for someone."

"Oh, really?" she asked and leaned in with interest. I got the feeling she spent most of her day explaining the copier fees to people and welcomed the chance to talk about anything else. "Do you have a name?"

"I don't," I said. "She has black hair and very blue eyes. I know she works on the first floor too, but that's all I know."

"That sounds like Madeline Evans. Are you in some kind of trouble?"

"No, why?" I asked.

"She's a state's attorney. Go through that door," the woman said and pointed to a door across the lobby. "It's down that hall to the left. You'll see the sign."

"Thank you so much," I said.

"You're welcome. You sure you don't need any copies?"

"I'm sure. Thanks again."

I made my way across the lobby and went through the door the information lady had pointed to. It opened into a narrow hallway that reminded me of something in an old hospital. There was light blue tile halfway up the walls and the top portion was painted in a faded ecru. I could even swear I smelled antiseptic, but that might have been some sort of memory triggered by the hallway's appearance.

Most of the way down the hall, I found a door that said "State's Attorney". Inside was a small waiting area and a counter with a Plexiglas enclosure extending from the top of the counter to the ceiling. It didn't seem like the kind of thing that would be necessary in a small town like Coventry, but maybe it was the kind of thing that was necessary everywhere.

There was one man seated in the waiting area and he was absorbed with his phone. I approached the counter, and a younger woman with red glasses and her hair piled on top her head in a large messy bun greeted me.

"Can I help you?" she asked.

"Yes, I need to see Madeline Evans," I said.

"Do you have an appointment?"

"I don't, but I want to talk to her about the Merrill Killian murder."

"Give me a moment," the girl said and stood up. "I'll see if she's available. What's your name?"

"Kinsley Skeenbauer," I said.

The woman disappeared into the offices beyond the counter. I could see a couple of doors, but I had no idea how many were actually back there. The area turned into another hallway on either side.

She reappeared a couple of minutes later. "She said she's got a few minutes. You can go on back."

The woman pressed a button and there was a button sound. I figured it was for the door to my left, so I tried it and it opened. I walked around behind the counter and stood in front of the woman in red glasses' desk.

"Which office is hers?"

"To the right. There's a plaque," she said.

It wasn't hard to find, but the door was closed. I knocked once and heard someone say "come in."

The office was large, and Madeline was seated behind a huge mahogany desk. To the left of her L-shaped desk was a small conference table and six chairs. On the back wall behind her was a huge white board. At the time, it was blank. The only other decoration on the walls was a picture of a cabin in the woods. Calling it a cabin was kind of an understatement. It was a huge two-story log home next to a beautiful blue pond.

"Have a seat," she said.

I sat down at the conference table, and Madeline joined me. There was a stack of legal pads and a cup of pens in the center, but she didn't grab one right away.

"You said you wanted to talk to me about Merrill's death?" she began. "Do you have information?"

"I don't, but I heard that he was supposed to meet with you," I said. "I was hoping you might be able to tell me something."

She studied me for a moment. "I wouldn't be able to tell you about a case," she said. "How did you hear about this?"

It was right then that I realized I had no cover story. I'd heard about it from his ghost, but I couldn't very well tell her about that.

"Small town. Stuff gets around," I said with a shrug.

Madeline eyed me skeptically. "I very much doubt that got around given that he was coming to me because he was worried about even going to the sheriff. But I don't have any idea how you know because I don't know what he wanted. He never made it in that day to talk to me. As you probably know, he died. Maybe you could end up helping me. If you're poking around and you find out why he wanted to see me," she said and turned around to grab a business card off her desk, "I'd like it if you called me." She slid the business card across the table to me. "Does the sheriff know you've got your nose in this?"

"I think he has his suspicions, but I've managed to mostly steer clear of him," I said.

"Can I ask why you're involved?" Madeline asked.

"Because I found the body and so far, I'm basically the main suspect. I just moved back here, and I'd like for everyone to stop thinking I'm a murderer."

"That's what I thought," she said. "You're Amelda's great-granddaughter, right?"

"I am," I said.

"You should know that's the only reason I agreed to see you, and it's the only reason I'm not going to look harder at why you're involved in this. Keep your nose clean and don't ruffle Thorn's feathers. I don't want to have to step in."

"Yes, ma'am," I said.

"And don't call me ma'am again," she said with a laugh. "Is there anything else I can do for you? I've got a meeting with my boss upstate in two hours."

"Is that where the cabin is?" I said, not able to take my eyes off the gorgeous house and landscape. "I mean, is it upstate or is it around here? I can't recall ever seeing such a gorgeous house. Sorry, I'm being nosy. I love that photo."

"It is upstate. That's where I lived before they moved me to Coventry. I still own the place, but I've thought about selling. I'm just too busy to get up there much anymore. Plus, there's not much around it. My parents built it thinking the town it's close to, Norman, was going to get built up. It didn't. So, it's a pain to spend much time there because it's isolated, but sometimes that's just what a person needs."

"That's too bad. It's a gorgeous place."

"It is. Okay, well I do have to go. Anything else?" Madeline asked.

"Nope, thank you," I said. "I can show myself out."

Meri was still on top of the trailer napping in the sun when I got back. There was also a man I didn't recognize walking down the street in my direction. I assumed he was a tourist until he stopped right in front of the shop.

"Are you Kinsley?" he asked as I came around the trailer.

"I am," I said bracing for someone else to tell me I was a murderer, and I needed to get out of town.

"I'm Jacob Winemaker. One of Castor's properties is across the street from one of mine over in that new subdivision, Cherry Heights. Anyway, he got held up there with a big plumbing thing and asked me to bring you this key. I'm on my way to the courthouse to pull some permits, and I told him I could stop by," he said and produced a key. "He said he'd get you the other copies as soon as he can."

"Thank you," I said and took the key. "Hey, you were the landlord of the guy that rented this shop before me."

"Yeah, Lance Bleucastle. He skipped out on me and Castor. That's actually how we became friends," Jacob said. "And you're the woman who found Merrill Killian's body. You know, a lot of people say you killed him."

"I've heard that," I said and rolled my eyes.

Jacob laughed. "Hey, I didn't like that guy at all. He owed me a lot of money, but I guess that's the case with a lot of people. He was supposed to pay me back by selling his house to me on the cheap, but he backed out of the deal when the guy he was supposed to rent a trailer from figured out that he was broke and had terrible credit. I suppose it's my own fault for putting myself in a position where Merrill owed me money. I should have known better."

"It sounds like he duped a lot of people," I said.

"He did, but I'm going to get that house one way or another. Now that Merrill is dead, his estate will have to sell it to pay off the lien Jerry Sprigs put on it. Since there's no mortgage, they might even sell it for the amount of the lien, so I could still cash in on this. It's like it's a win-win for everyone. Well, except Merrill, but whatever. That dude sucked."

I was a little taken aback, but I tried to keep it from showing on my face. "So, you really didn't like the guy," I said.

"Yeah, I didn't, but I didn't hate him enough to kill him. I know that's what you're thinking. I've heard you've been asking around. Too bad you got stuck with that hanging around your neck."

"Do you know anybody that might have hated him enough to kill him?" I asked. "Everyone seemed to have disliked him a whole lot, but nobody cared enough to put their lives on the line to take him out. I guess I need to find someone that hated him so much that they'd be willing to take the risk."

"He had a girlfriend, you know? Pretty thing that was way too young for him, but she's not very bright. Obviously if she went for the likes of Merrill. Anyway, I heard he was really mean to her and maybe even got her hooked on meth."

"Merrill was into meth too?" I couldn't believe it.

"Dude like that was into a lot of things," Jacob said. "Anyway, her brother probably hated Merrill enough to kill him. He did not like his baby sister being treated that way."

"Who is she?" I asked. "And who is the brother?"

"Her name's Katy Shoals. Brother's name is Kevin," Jacob said. "He's a construction worker."

"Hey, thanks," I said.

"Yeah, you're welcome. But, hey. Kevin Shoals has kind of a reputation for being a hard... for being a tough guy. So, watch yourself around him. He's not someone to mess with," Jacob said.

"I will. I swear. Tell Castor I said thanks for the key."

"Will do."

With the key in hand, I went into the shop and looked around. Immediately, the scratching on the bathroom door started again.

"Meri, we're going to have to do something about that before I open the shop. It doesn't scare me, but it might freak the tourists out," I said.

"Isn't that what they want?" he asked.

"That's a good point." I said.

"Besides, it will probably stop when there are customers in the shop. You know ghosts rarely show themselves when you'd be able to use their presence to confirm a haunting," he said.

"Why is that?" I asked.

"I don't know, but if you want to banish it, we can. Or you could wait and see if it shows itself. See what it wants."

"I'll probably just do that. It's more annoying than anything at this point," I said and walked to the back of the store. "Hey, knock it off or my familiar and I are going to banish your spectral behind," I shouted through the door.

"Good job," Meri said when it stopped.

With the ghost at least temporarily taken care of, I propped the front door open and started carrying in boxes. I got them all out of the trailer and carried inside when I realized something was missing.

"What is it?" Meri asked as I stood inside biting my bottom lip and thinking.

"I need a sign for the store," I said. "I could probably paint something with temporary window paint on the outside for a while, but eventually, I'll need a sign."

"You have enough money to order one," Meri said.

"I know, but I don't have enough money in my account. The only bank in Coventry is the Bank of Coventry, right?"

"Yeah."

"So, I can't deposit any of this money into my other account," I said. "I'll have to open an account here and wait for a debit card."

"You should go soon then. Get there before they close, or you'll have to wait until tomorrow," Meri said.

"I don't need to go right now. I should have time."

"It's nearly four," Meri said.

"Really? Wow, this all took longer than I thought. Okay. I should do that and then I've got to get home and get ready for my date with Thorn."

I ended up leaving the trailer parked outside the shop because while there was a small branch of the bank near the square, the big new branch out in the new section of town said they could make me a debit card for my new account right then and there. Meri and I got in the car and headed off to a part of town I'd never been in before. In fact, it had been all farm fields when I'd left.

The bank was conveniently located in a small business and retail area before you got to the subdivisions. I pulled into the parking lot and parked near the doors. Meri was going to wait in the car, but there were some interesting bushes around the building. He decided to get out and investigate the landscaping while I did my banking.

There was only one other customer in the bank when I went inside. I walked up to the teller and told her I wanted to open a checking account with a debit card.

"Sure, I can do that," she said. "Or if you want to discuss your options, you can have a seat and I'll tell one of our personal bankers you are here."

"No, that's fine. I just want a standard checking account with a debit card," I said.

Chapter Fourteen

Twenty minutes later I had my new bank account and debit card. I hadn't had much cash on me to deposit in the account, but I'd had just enough to open it. I'd have to go back the next day with more.

That was a problem for another time. At that moment, I needed to get home and get ready for my date with Thorn. I'd have over an hour by the time I got there, and I reasoned that was plenty of time. Especially for a witch.

My first order of business when I arrived at Hangman's House was to feed Meri his dinner. My second was to get in the shower and thoroughly scrub off the day's worth of dust and sweat that had caked over my entire body. I scrubbed and exfoliated everything until my skin was a little red but also as smooth as a baby's butt.

The one thing my ex hadn't taken from me was my collection of soaps, lotions, and my makeup. For special occasions, I had a gardenia lotion that smelled like absolute heaven. At a hundred dollars a bottle, I save it for truly exceptional events. I pulled that bad boy out of my bag and slathered it all over myself. If I was going to make the mistake of jumping into something with the town's hunky sheriff way too fast, I was going to pull out all the stops.

I had to decide between doing the no-makeup makeup look or going all out with a glam smoky eye. I wasn't a shifter, but I could shape shift with makeup. I hoped he wasn't taking me to the diner for dinner because I went with the smoky eye and blood-red lips. I had the perfect little black dress that showed off just enough skin, a little shoulder and a hint of thigh, without giving away too much. Since it displayed my shoulders, I applied a bit of highlighter to them so there was a bit of sparkle that caught the light. Not too much though. I knew we weren't going clubbing or to a carnival.

The pink in my hair had deepened to red and the purple was so dark it was almost black. I decided to blow dry it, curl it, and then wear it with the crown done up and the bottom layers loose. With the crown tied back, you could see my neck and get a good view of the little silver moon earrings that dangled about a half inch from my ear. They hung from tiny diamond studs that looked like stars.

"You look nice," Meri said as I emerged from the bathroom.

"What? Did you just pay me a compliment?" I was a little shocked.

"No. You're crazy. You must be hearing things," he said and darted out of the room.

"Whatever," I called out to him.

"Whatever," I heard back from somewhere downstairs.

Since I was ready to go, all there was left to do was wait for Thorn. I went downstairs and sat on the sofa thinking I could boot up my laptop and scroll through social media for a few minutes, but I couldn't sit still. I ended up pacing the living room until a few minutes before six when the doorbell rang. One thing I knew for sure was that my calves were going to hurt the next day after pacing in my heels.

I answered the door to an audible gasp. Thorn's mouth hung open for just a split second before he snapped it shut and tried to compose himself. He was dressed in black slacks that clung to his developed thighs and an eggplant purple dress button-down shirt that hugged his biceps and was slightly taut against his muscular chest. His blond hair was neatly combed but not overly so. One lock threatened to spill down over his forehead. Even after he recovered from his apparent shock at seeing me, his eyes still sparkled with mischievous delight.

"You look... I can't even say beautiful because that wouldn't describe it," he said and cleared his throat. "I just... I never expected..."

"Are you going to be okay, Sheriff?" I teased. "Do we need to call in one of your deputies for backup?"

"Will you marry me?" he said completely seriously.

"You're hilarious," I countered.

"Well, will you at least come out here so I can take you to dinner then?"

I would never know if he was serious in that moment. We both played it off as a joke, but he never did actually say he was kidding.

"Sure," I said and Thorn offered me his arm.

He walked me out to his truck. It was a huge, black behemoth with enormous tires and a lift kit. It wasn't exactly in monster truck territory, but it was... something.

"Sorry about the truck," he said as he opened the door for me and helped me into the cab. "My car is in the shop, and I didn't think you'd want me picking you up in my cruiser."

"Plus, I don't think you're supposed to use your cruiser for personal business," I teased.

"Yeah, that's right," he said as he shut my door.

I waited for him to come around and get in. "But thank you for not picking me up in it. I'm sure the entire town would have thought I was under arrest," I said once he was behind the wheel. "It's a nice truck."

"But a little over the top?" he asked.

"Maybe a little," I said.

"Well, it does serve a purpose occasionally when I need to go off road for things," Thorn said.

"How often do you have to do that?" I asked.

"Not often enough to justify having the beast," he said with a smile.

"That's okay. We all have our thing. I'd say of the list of vices I can think of, liking big trucks is pretty harmless."

"I'm glad to hear you say that," he said. "I worried you'd think I was some sort of country bumpkin when you saw it."

"Thorn, I'm the one that grew up in a small town. You're the one who grew up in the city. Besides, I'm not going to judge you over a truck."

With that, he reached across the console and took my hand. "I hope you like Italian food. If not, I can take you somewhere else."

"I love anything pasta," I said a little too enthusiastically.

Thorn chuckled. "That's what your mom told me."

"You asked my mom where to take me?" I asked.

"Yeah, and she said you'd love Bella Vita," he said. "I don't regret asking. I was a Boy Scout, and I'm always prepared."

"I saw Bella Vita when I was at the bank today. It looks like a fancy restaurant," I said.

"Well, it's a good thing you dressed the part," he said and squeezed my hand. "It is the nicest restaurant in Coventry."

I was glad I hadn't gone with a more casual outfit. "Would you have told me if you'd shown up and I was dressed in something less fancy?" I said.

"Not a chance. I would have taken you somewhere else and then taken you to Bella Vita on our next date," he said.

"Why?"

"Because I would never say anything even remotely negative to you about the way you're dressed, Kinsley. Not when I could just take you somewhere more casual and relaxed. Your outfit would have told me that's what you're in the mood for, and I am here to cater to that."

"But I'm dressed for Bella Vita," I said and squeezed his hand back.

"Kinsley, you're dressed for a five-star restaurant in the city. But is Bella Vita okay? I can drive us to Chicago. It will take a while."

"St. Louis is probably closer," I said.

"Good point. Do you want to go there?"

"No, I'm hungry," I said.

He laughed and had to let go of my hand so we could turn into the restaurant's parking lot. Once we were parked, Thorn came around and opened the door. He practically had to lift me out of the truck and help me to the ground. I was a little embarrassed at first. I just felt self-conscious about him having to pick me up.

"We need to get you inside stat," he said as he set me down.

"Why? I'm not cold. It's a nice night," I said.

"Because you hardly weigh anything, Kinsley. We need to get you full of pasta and bread sticks fast."

"Oh, now you're just trying to score points," I said and playfully hit his arm.

"Did it work?"

"It absolutely worked."

He offered me his hand and we walked to the door. Thorn held it open for me and then took my hand again as we waited at the hostess station.

"Reservation for Wilson," Thorn said when the hostess greeted us.

"You made a reservation today?" I said as she walked us to our table.

"I made a reservation the night I met you," he said. "Just in case."

"The night of the murder?" I was surprised.

"Yeah, I made it after I went home. Just in case," Thorn said.

"That was a bit presumptuous of you," I said, but I was still teasing.

"It may have been, but it paid off," Thorn said.

"Will this do?" the hostess asked as she showed us to a high-backed booth.

"Will it?" Thorn asked me, and I suddenly felt like a princess.

"Yes. It's great," I said with a smile.

"Yes, thank you," Thorn said to the hostess.

"Your server will be right with you," she said and walked away.

I slid into the booth and picked up the menu the hostess had left on my side of the table. The selections were listed in both Italian and English, so I was able to read the menu. I made a mental note to ask my father to do his language spell so I could speak and read Italian, though. It was a beautiful language, and I figured why not? My father had the ability, so I might as well take advantage.

The menu was extensive, and I studied it with focus while we waited for the waitress to come take our orders. I really was hungry, and I didn't want to have to send her away. Thorn was as intense in his perusal of their selection as I was. It was nice to see we were on the same page in that regard.

"Are you going to think less of me if I get the spaghetti with meat sauce?" Thorn asked after a couple of minutes.

"Why would I think less of you for that?" I asked.

"Well, I brought you to such a fancy place and then I order something so basic," he said.

"I'm sure it's not basic here," I offered. "I bet they've elevated it to something magical."

"Well, when you put it that way," he said.

His eyes twinkled in the soft light from the candle in the middle of the table. The flame threw a shadow across his jaw and made it look even more chiseled as it lit up the blond stubble he'd neglected to shave.

"Do I have something on my face?" he asked.

"Oh, no. Sorry. I was just..."

He rubbed his jaw. "Sorry, I guess I should have shaved."

"No, it's a good look on you," I said. "Very rugged. Goes with the truck."

He laughed at that. "Well, wait until you see me outside in my flannel chopping fire wood."

"People still do that?" I asked.

That time Thorn let out a huge belly laugh. "They do if they have a wood-burning fireplace or stove. I happen to have both in my house. I suppose I could buy one of those machines that does it for you, but the exercise is good for me," he said and patted his stomach.

"That it is," I said and then blushed furiously.

"Thank you," he said and blushed a little too. That made me feel better.

The waitress came right then and took our orders. Thorn did go with the spaghetti and meat sauce. I decided on the spaghetti aglio e olio. We also ordered an extra basket of bread with olive oil and herbs to dip it in.

While we were eating our bread, I brought the investigation up. I tried to talk myself out of it, but I was coming out of my skin. "So, how is the investigation into Merrill's murder going?" I asked and then held my breath.

"I think I should probably be asking you that?" Thorn said. He was smiling, but there was an edge to his voice.

"What I'm mostly finding out is that Merrill owed a lot of people money and that he was not well liked. Did you know that Jerry Sprigs is putting a lien on Merrill's estate for twelve grand?"

"I'd ask how you know that, but I think I already know," Thorn said.

"What do you mean?" I asked as innocently as possible.

"Look, Kinsley, I can't prove you went into Merrill's house, and I don't want to accuse you of things, but if you did, please don't do anything like that again. Don't put me in a position where I have to arrest you. Please?"

"You know you want me in handcuffs," I said to lighten the mood.

He let out some sort of low, rumbly growl that took my breath away. "Anyway..." Thorn began after rubbing the back of his neck and clearing his throat again, "I'm going to track down my contact in Azriel's club. I think I'd like to know what they've found out so far. They haven't come to you, have they?"

"No," I said. "If they did, I would tell you."

"Good."

I wanted to ask him if I could come along when he talked to his contact, but I chickened out. I didn't think he'd be amenable to the idea, so there was no reason to upset him over it.

Our food came after that, so we ate and chatted over far less intense topics. When dinner was over, he drove me home and walked me to my door.

"Thank you for dinner," I said. "It was delicious. The company was okay too."

Thorn chuckled. "I'm glad you enjoyed it. The food especially. I've never seen a woman eat like that before," he said and thought about it. "I take that back. I've seen your mother eat like that when your folks have been gracious enough to invite me to dinner. It's a good quality for you to have inherited."

"I'm glad it didn't horrify you," I said.

Thorn studied me for a moment. "Everything about you makes me like you more," he finally said.

"Oh, well, you'll get over that quick enough."

"Don't deflect me with humor, Kinsley," he said seriously. "If you don't like me, fine, but don't do that."

"I'm not... I mean... I'm not doing that," I stammered. "I do like you. More than I should, probably." I bit my bottom lip hard. "Dang it. I didn't mean to say that out loud. I'm sorry."

"And don't apologize for telling me the truth," he said. Thorn wrapped his arms around my waist and pulled me close. "And don't abuse that gorgeous bottom lip that way."

Before I could respond, Thorn pulled me in closer and covered my lips with his. I just melted into him and breathed in his clean, woodsy aftershave. The stubble on his chin sent a shiver down my spine.

"Are you cold?" he pulled back and asked.

"No, not at all."

Chapter Fifteen

The next morning I went to the bank and deposited a bunch of money Meri found for me in the attic. "You know, you're a really great familiar," I said as we were driving home.

"Shut up," he retorted.

"No, I'm serious," I said. "I know serving as our familiar was a punishment. Well, back when my mother wasn't a Skeenbauer anyway. But you've been good to us. A little snarky, but you've saved us all so many times."

"What are you getting at?" he asked suspiciously.

"Maybe you should be rewarded for your service," I said. "Has anyone ever rewarded you for your service to the coven?"

"Well, I mean, up until your mother married into the Skeenbauer coven, she basically *was* the coven," Meri said.

"I'm still a Tuttlesmith witch," I said. "My last name is Skeenbauer, but that doesn't change that half of my lineage is still with the other coven. But that's not the point. The point is that I want to do something nice for you."

"Like what? Are you going to turn into a genie and grant me a wish?" he asked sarcastically.

"I don't think you can just turn into a Jinn," I said. "And even if I could, I'm not sure that's who you want granting your wishes."

"So, are we talking like extra bacon and salmon then?" Meri asked hopefully.

"Well, that too. But not just that. I can't become a Jinn, but I'm supposed to be the most powerful witch in the world or whatever. I can do a ritual to grant you a wish."

"Uh oh," Meri said.

"What? You don't want a wish?"

"You're serious."

"I'm totally serious. Are you in?" I asked.

"What? We're like doing this now?" Meri asked.

"Yeah. Let's do this now. Even you think I need to get back into doing magic. So, let's do some magic."

"Don't you want to open the store?"

"I want to wait until we get the sign," I said. "It's pretty much set up other than that. I'll do a grand opening or something after the new sign comes and it's installed."

"You haven't ordered a sign," Meri protested.

"I can do that after we grant your wish," I said.

"I can just wish for a sign."

"Meri."

"Kinsley."

"Come on. Don't be a scaredy-cat," I said.

"What, are you daring me to do this?"

"Yes," I said.

"Fine."

We went home, and I pushed all of the furniture out of the center of the living room. After drawing a giant pentagram in the middle of the floor with white chalk, I collected all of my red and white candles. Those were arranged around the edge of the circle, and in between them I drew sigils for wish fulfillment.

When that was done, I lit the candles and Meri and I stepped into the circle. "I'm not sure if I should be in here with you," I said. "I think I'm going to draw a bigger circle around this one, and I'll stand inside that."

"It's your rodeo," Meri responded.

I took the chalk and drew the circle around the pentagram. Once that was done, I sealed the outer circle with a line of salt and placed rose quartz obelisks and spheres next to each cluster of candles.

I had parchment paper and a dragon's blood ink pen already ready to go. I also had a black marker and a bay leaf.

"Okay, we're going for the double whammy on this one," I said. "I'm going to write your wish on parchment in the dragon's blood ink. I'm also going to write it on the bay leaf with the black marker. You focus on your wish. I'll burn the bay leaf first and then I'll burn the parchment."

"That's it?" Meri asked.

"I think that should just about do it. We could do an older, more complicated ritual, but this is all it takes. The candles and rose quartz will augment the magic, and so will your intentions. Why, did you want something with chanting and summoning of spirits? I can do that too," I said.

"No, this is fine," he said.

"Okay, so tell me your wish," I said.

"Do I have to?" he asked.

"Well, you could dip your paw in dragon's blood ink and press it to the page," I said. "Same with the bay leaf."

"Yeah, let's do that."

"Okay," I said.

I'd kept a bag of supplies inside the circle just in case, and I had a vial of dragon's blood ink. I took it out and carefully poured some on Meri's paw. He put his print down on the paper, and then I used the marker to cover the pads on his other paw. He pressed that one to the bay leaf.

"All right. I'm going to burn them now. Are you ready to stay focused on your wish?"

"Got it. It's in my head. Let's do this."

I burned the bay leaf first. I knew to keep the smoke away from my face as it could be hallucinogenic.

"Don't suck too much of that in," Meri said.

"Hey, you keep your mind on your wish," I said. "So, is anything happening? I don't know what you wished for, so I don't know if it's working."

"It's tingling a little," he said.

"Okay."

"So, do the parchment, I guess."

"All right. I'm going to burn the parchment now. Keep your mind focused."

I lit the parchment and held it out in front of me until it had burned close enough to singe my fingers. When the flame got too close, I dropped it into a little copper offering bowl.

"Anything?" I asked as the flame consumed the last little bit of paper.

Before he could answer, purple smoke came up through the pentagram and surrounded Meri. "I'd say it's working," he said and then sneezed.

"Are you all right in there?" I asked when the smoke got so thick I couldn't see him anymore.

"I'm fine," he said, but there was something off about his voice.

"Meri?"

"It's me," he said, but his voice was so much higher pitched than it had been before.

The smoke finally cleared, and I couldn't believe my eyes. Meri had turned into a tiny black kitten.

"What?!?!" he shrieked when he realized what had happened.

"I take it you didn't wish to be a kitten?" I asked cautiously.

"No!!!!" he hollered, but his voice was so small and cute that it made me laugh.

"What did you wish for then?" I asked.

"Not this!"

"You might as well tell me now. Maybe I can fix it?"

"Oh, no. You're not casting any more spells on me, Kinsley Skeenbauer. What have you done?"

"I granted your wish," I said. "So, what was it? Just tell me."

"I've always felt a little guilty about some of the choices I've made in this life. I wanted a fresh start. I wanted a clean slate to try and do better."

"Really?" I was in disbelief. "I never would have guessed you ever felt guilty about anything."

"Ha ha," he said. "What have you done?"

"I mean... this is a fresh start, right? Technically. Maybe you should have been a little more specific," I offered.

"I can't believe this," he said.

"You're kind of adorable."

"Oh my gawd. Shut up. You're loving this, aren't you?"

"No, of course not," I said.

"Can you change it back?" he asked.

"I mean, I can try if you really want me to," I said.

"No. Nope. Uh uh. No way. I'm going to go see your mother. Maybe she and your father can fix this."

"Okay," I said. "Are you going to come back?" I walked to the front door and opened it for him.

"Probably," he said and then darted out into the night.

I waited up for him to come back. For a while I was able to distract myself by shopping online for a sign for the store. Eventually, my mom sent me a text letting me know that Meri was on his way back.

Did you fix him? I asked.

He's still a kitten. :-) Don't worry, he'll get over it. she responded.

Thanks, Mom. For trying to help, I mean. I said.

Hey, you gave him what he wanted. He'll be fine. I promise. Now get some rest. I'm going to bed. she responded.

I waited a little while longer, and then there was finally a scratching at the front door. I let Meri in and he ran upstairs without a word. Not only was he still a kitten, but I thought it was possible he was even smaller than I remembered. Had my mother done that, or was it just my imagination playing tricks on me?

When I went upstairs, I found him curled up on the bed. He didn't say anything to me, but I took it as a good sign he wasn't hiding.

He still didn't speak to me after I'd brushed my teeth and changed my pajamas. I wondered how long I'd be on the receiving end of the silent treatment.

Chapter Sixteen

The next morning, I fed Meri, and while he did eat, he still wasn't talking to me. I'd ordered a sign while I was waiting for him, but it would be a couple of days until it came. I felt myself growing restless at the idea of sitting around the house all day.

Instead, I decided to track down Kevin Shoals and talk to him about his sister, Katy. Well, more about how much he hated Merrill Killian, but I would lead into the conversation with his sister.

I remembered that Jacob said Kevin was a construction worker. That meant the most likely place to find him was in one of the new housing developments.

I got in my car and drove over to the first one I encountered. Only about every third house was completed in Blossom Fields, so it wasn't hard to find one with men working. I parked my car along the closest thing to resemble a curb I could find and walked up to the first man I saw who wasn't swinging a hammer or lifting something heavy.

"Excuse me?" I said as I tapped him on the shoulder.

"You need a hard hat," he grumbled.

"I just have a quick question," I said. "And then I will be on my way."

"Make it fast."

"I'm looking for Kevin Shoals. Is he working at this site?" I asked hopefully.

"Kevin doesn't work for this company anymore. He's on the crew over in Lilac Meadows. Oh, no, wait, he's over in Weeping Willows. Number thirteen, I think. I'm not sure. You just go over there and ask around. You'll find him."

"Thank you," I said. "I appreciate it."

"No problem," he said and turned back to what he'd been doing.

I got back in my car and drove down the main road until I got to The Weeping Willows. Some of the house numbers were spray painted on the street, so I had a fairly easy time finding number thirteen.

Number thirteen was barely in the beginning stages of being built, so all the men were working outside. It also meant I had to park my car way down the block and walk as there were several pieces of heavy equipment in the street.

"I'm looking for Kevin Shoals," I said to a man who was climbing into a large digging machine thing.

"Right there," he said and pointed to a guy who was talking to another man. The other man looked like he might be some sort of supervisor, I could tell by his clothes and lack of dirt, so I hung back until they were done talking.

"Hey, Kevin?" I said once he was alone again.

"Who are you?" he asked me flatly.

"My name is Kinsley Skeenbauer. I wanted to talk to you about your sister and Merrill Killian," I said.

"Why would I talk to you about that?" he asked gruffly.

"Because right now, I'm a suspect. You're a suspect, and so is your sister. I'd like to clear that up for all of us if I could."

"So, what are you? Some sort of private detective?"

"No, I'm the one who found Merrill's body at the diner. I'm really kind of the main suspect, and I want to figure out who killed him. That way I'm not the main suspect anymore."

"So, you think I did it?" he asked.

"I mean, you did hate him, right? You hated him because he wasn't good to your sister? That seems like a pretty good reason for a big brother to go a little homicidal," I said. "But I'm not here to accuse you. I just want the truth, and if I think it's possible you did it, it's only a matter of time before the sheriff comes around asking."

"Fine. I've got a break coming to me. I suppose I don't mind spending it with you," he said. "Let me grab my soda from my cooler. I'll be right back."

A minute later he reappeared with a bottle of Coke and a pack of cigarettes. He took out a cigarette and lit it before taking a long drink of the Coke.

"Yeah, I hated the guy," he said as he exhaled another drag of smoke.

"I've heard it was because he wasn't good to your sister," I said.

'That's an understatement. The guy was abusive. I was raised that you never put your hands on a woman," he said.

"So, he hit her," I said.

'That I'm not sure of, but I know he shoved her and threw things at her. That's all she would admit to," he said and inhaled half his cigarette in one go. "But that's enough for me."

"You did something to him?" I asked.

"Heck, yeah. I kicked his... butt. But, Katy still wouldn't leave him. In fact, she took his side. She wouldn't even talk to me for a while, but I don't regret it."

"That must have been tough," I said.

"And then it got worse when he got her using drugs," Jacob said and rubbed the back of his neck. "She was a good girl until she met Merrill. Heck, he was like twenty years older than her, and he just corrupted her. It's not like he had money for those drugs either, so Katy was the one buying them for him. She nearly lost her job at the groomer's over it."

"She works at the groomers? Paws and Claws?"

"That's the one. College wasn't in Katy's future. Heck, it wasn't in mine either, obviously, but she did get her groomer's license and the owner gave her a chance. She's good. I've tried to convince her a few times to go get her cosmetology license from the beauty school so she can make more money doing people's hair, but Katy loves working with the dogs."

"She sounds like a sweet woman," I said.

"She really is, but she's too nice. That's what got her mixed up with the likes of Merrill Killian. Don't take this the wrong way, but I'm glad he's gone. My sister is heartbroken now, but at least she's got a chance to find a good man."

"Shoals!" a burly man called from the job site.

"I have to go," Kevin said. "I hope I cleared some things up for you, and I hope you figure out who did this. It's terrible that you're caught up in all this. I'm pretty good at reading people, and you're no killer."

He turned to leave after that, so I went back to my car. I believed Kevin when he said he didn't kill Merrill. That was good for him, but it left me down another suspect. I wasn't any closer to clearing my name.

Chapter Seventeen

While I was driving, I decided that there were a few things in my shop I wanted to rearrange. The items that would appeal more to tourists needed to be closer to the front while things only real witches would want needed to be all the way into the store. I also remembered seeing a bunch of unused Mason jars in the basement storage and thought it would be a good idea to fill them with some graveyard dirt to sell. Graveyard dirt was good for a lot of things, but most witches didn't want to be caught collecting it. Not that it was illegal, but regular people thought it was weird.

Before I went into the shop, though, I decided to stop by the house and see if Meri was ready to talk to me yet. When I got to Hangman's House, I went inside and he was sitting on the sofa watching the door.

"What?" he asked.

"I was going to go into the shop for a bit. Thought I'd stop by and see if you wanted to join me."

"Fine," he said and jumped off the sofa.

"Are you okay?"

"I don't want to talk about it," he said as he sort of skittered over to me. "For gawd's sake, I can't even walk without looking like an idiot."

"It's cute," I said.

"Shut up."

"Plus, when I take you places, we don't need as big of a bag anymore. You're like a little ninja now."

"I hate you," Meri said.

"I hate you too," I said as I picked him up and brought him up to my shoulder.

"I can walk just fine," he snarked.

"I know. Just let me have this," I said.

"Fine, but I still hate you," he said and pressed his little kitten head to my collarbone.

We got to the store, and I called the company I'd rented the trailer from to see if they could just come pick it up. The guy on the phone told me there would be an extra charge for that, but since I wasn't really broke anymore, I agreed to it. I gave him my debit card number and then proceeded to start moving things around on the shelves the way I'd envisioned them.

I'd been there for around an hour when Castor showed up. "Hey, this is really coming together already," he said from the doorway.

"You can come in," I said. "It's okay, I promise."

"I'm fine here," he said. "I've got those keys if you want to come grab them." He really wasn't going to come any further into the store.

"Okay, thanks," I said. "It really is fine, though."

Just as I said that, there was a loud noise like a pop from the bathroom in the back. That sound was followed by the babble of rushing water.

I ran into the back to find that something was broken on the toilet and it was spraying water everywhere. Water was already starting to pool on the tile floor.

"Oh, no!"

"What is it?" Castor shouted from his place by the door.

"Toilet's broken. There's water everywhere," I called back. I almost panicked, but then I remembered I was a witch... "Wait, I think I can fix it." I tried to sound convincing.

I could fix it, but I didn't want Castor to catch me using magic. I was about to use magic to shut the water off when Castor said something again. He was closer too. Apparently, a broken toilet was all it took to overcome his fear of the ghost who had probably done this.

"I'm going to shut the water off for now," Castor said. "Let me do that, and then I'll call Jerry Sprigs. He owes me a favor. I'll get him in here to fix this today."

"I can do it, really," I said.

"No," he said as he walked toward the door. I assumed the water shutoff was outside, but I really didn't know. "I'm the landlord. This is my issue to deal with, Kinsley."

"Okay," I relented. "Thank you."

A couple of minutes later, the water shut off. Castor reappeared in the doorway of the shop. I really needed to get a bell to go over the door.

"I called Jerry. He's working on a job right now, but he'll be by later this afternoon. Call me and let me know if he doesn't make it," Castor said.

"Thank you, I appreciate it," I said.

"You going to stay here and keep working, or do I need to get him a key?" Castor asked.

"I'll be here. If I need to use the restroom, I'll go across the square and see if Viv will let me use hers," I said.

"She's a good girl. I'm sure she will," Castor said. "In fact, I think I'll go over there and get myself a coffee and one of those pecan tortes."

"Enjoy," I said. "And thanks again for the keys."

I went about my business rearranging the shelves, and around lunchtime, Jerry showed up. "Hello," he called out as he came through the door.

Suddenly, I felt uncomfortable being alone with him in the shop. "Oh, hi, Jerry. I was just heading out for an errand. I didn't expect to see you until later this afternoon," I said.

"Yeah, I just had lunch. I wanted to go ahead and get your issue dealt with before I go back to my other job," he said.

"Okay, well, I'll leave you to it. I'll be back in a little while," I said and made my way over to the door. I grabbed my purse on my way past a pyramid of boxes I still needed to break down.

"Bathroom's in the back?" he asked.

"It is. Thanks again," I said and went outside before he had a chance to say anything else.

I'd only seen the breakfast menu at the Brew Station, but I decided to chance that they might have something for lunch. Meri had followed me out, so I stuck him in my purse. He couldn't protest because there were people around, but his eyes as I closed the zipper most of the way told me everything I needed to know. I wouldn't have been surprised if he'd used the magical energy to poof himself back to Hangman's House and just left me alone for the rest of the day.

The Brew Station did have a selection of cold sandwiches available for lunch. The place was packed, though, so I didn't get a chance to talk to Viv. She smiled at me, but she and her helper were frantically trying to fill orders.

I got a sandwich with pepperoni, salami, ham, provolone, and Italian dressing with a hazelnut Italian soda to drink. There weren't any tables available unless I wanted to try to sit with someone else, so I took my meal to-go and went outside.

There were some benches open, so I sat down and opened my purse to let Meri out. He seemed disgruntled, but I was slightly forgiven when I shared my ham with him.

We sat and watched the tourists until Jerry emerged from my shop. He looked around for me, so I threw my trash in the bin and hurried across the street.

"Oh, there you are," he said.

"Yeah, sorry. I spaced out. How did it go?"

"Well, it's pretty much fixed. I'm going to turn the water back on so you can use it, but try to use it as little as possible. There's a part I need. I think I'm going to have to order one, so I'll be back in a couple of days," Jerry said.

"Okay, well, I should be around. You can have Castor call me if I'm not," I said.

"Will do." He looked like he wanted to say more, and I tried not to cringe. I was not looking forward to him making a pass at me. "Well, I have to go. I've got to get back to my other job."

I thanked him and then the Universe. At least I wouldn't have to worry about him again for a couple of days. I decided I'd also tell Castor about my discomfort with Jerry and see if there was someone else we could call. Or I'd just fix stuff myself from then on. Next time I had a problem, I'd keep my mouth shut and just deal with it.

Another couple of hours went by, and I got things just the way I wanted them. I was about to head out when the door opened again.

"I'm not open," I called out from the back of the store.

"But I was hoping you could teach me a love spell!" Reggie's voice called back.

"Oh, hi. It's good to see you," I said and made my way to the front. "How are you?"

"I'm doing okay," she said and picked up a rose quartz heart that was in a wooden bowl on one of the first shelves. "So, can I do a love spell? Do you know about that stuff? Or are you just selling souvenirs to tourists?"

"You can technically do a love spell, but I don't recommend it. Messing with other people's free will is a way to get yourself in deep with bad energy," I said.

"Well, that's a bummer," she said and put the heart back. "I bet you're going to get asked that a lot."

"I can imagine," I said. "But you can do a drawing spell to bring your true love to you. You just can't really force that role on anyone."

"Oh, so how much for the heart?" she said and picked it up again.

"You can have it," I said with a happy laugh. "I hope it brings much joy and love into your life."

"Why do I feel like you just cast a spell on me?" Reggie asked as she narrowed her eyes to study me.

"Probably because you're standing in a witch shop holding what you hope is an enchanted item, and we're talking about casting spells," I said with a shrug, but I had just cast a small spell on her.

"Yeah, that's probably it," she said and shrugged too.

But I could tell she didn't completely buy it. Some people could see through the magical veil over Coventry that was supposed to prevent them from picking up on the magical stuff going on around them. Reggie was one who could obviously see better than most.

"So, what brings you in?" I changed the subject. "Did you just want to check the shop out?"

"No, I actually have information," she said excitedly. "It could be a clue."

"What is it?" I asked.

"Hey, can we go outside and take a walk or something? Maybe go grab a coffee at Viv's place? I don't know what it is, but it feels like something is watching us here. I know that's crazy, but it's kinda freaky."

"It is supposed to be haunted," I said.

"I think this place actually is," she said and headed for the door.

We each got a latte at the Brew Station and headed back to my car. Reggie still hadn't told me her information yet, but she said she'd tell me on the way.

"On the way to where?" I asked as we got in my car.

"Oh, I was hoping you could give me a ride home," she said.

"Sure."

While I drove Reggie to her house, she started telling me her story. "So, my grandmother had some sort of breakdown because of her meds getting changed by some idiot doctor. Anyway, I've been spending a lot of time there the last couple of days to help her adjust."

"At Shady Acres?" I asked.

"Yes, and while I was out in the visitor's area getting her a soda and some chips from one of the machines, I heard a friend of Katy Shoals' grandmother gossiping about Katy. She was talking about how someone had seen Katy recently and she'd dyed her hair black. The woman said she thought it was so strange that Katy dyed her hair black for the funeral. She'd heard of people wearing black but never doing that to her hair."

"That is a little weird," I said. "I don't know if it's a clue."

"That's not all, though. I went and found Katy's grandmother. She lives at Shady Acres too, and she told me that Katy dyed her hair way before Merrill died. She said she hated it and didn't understand why her granddaughter had ruined her beautiful blonde hair that way. It could be something, right?" Reggie asked hopefully.

"I mean, it could be. I just don't know what," I said.

"We'll figure it out," Reggie said as I pulled into her driveway. "Hey, I'd invite you in, but I have to get ready for work."

"Do you need a ride?" I offered.

"No, the night cook is swinging by here on his way. He's going to give me a ride, but thank you," she said.

"You're welcome," I said. "And hey, I'll let you know if I figure anything out about the hair."

Chapter Eighteen

I went home after taking Reggie to her place and took a bath followed by a nap. When I woke up, it was dark and I was starving. Apparently, Meri was too because I woke up to him pawing my nose with his tiny toe beans.

"You can't even be a pain without being adorable anymore," I said and sat up.

"I just want salmon," he said. "We don't have to talk."

"I'll get you some salmon," I said and got up off the bed. "I'm going to make myself some dinner too."

After giving Meri a piece of fresh salmon and two strips of precooked bacon, I got out the bread and cheese to make myself a grilled cheese sandwich. There was a bag of those little fish crackers in the pantry, so I grabbed those too. I decided to round out the meal with a cup of creamy tomato soup.

I pulled the whole thing together in ten minutes, and I was so hungry that I probably ate it all in five. As I was cleaning up after myself, someone rang my doorbell. I thought perhaps it was Thorn, so I checked my phone. There was nothing from him saying he was coming over, so I went to the door and looked out the peephole.

My heart started to pound when I saw Azriel Malum standing on my porch. I wasn't sure if I was afraid or excited to see him. I really hated the effect he had on me, but at the same time, I reached for the doorknob and turned.

"Hello," I said when I opened the door.

That same wide smile that showed off his teeth and somehow lit his black eyes stretched across his face. "Good evening, Kinsley."

I cleared my throat and took a deep breath to calm my thundering heart. "What can I do for you?"

"You could invite me in," he said hypnotically.

"Oh, is that a real thing?" I asked warily.

"For us pure bloods it is," he said. "So, won't you invite me in?"

I should have shut the door or at least stepped out onto the porch, but my mouth betrayed my brain. "Please come in," I said. After all, what harm could he really do to me?

"Thank you," he said and stepped over the threshold.

"Pure bloods?" I asked as I walked to my sofa.

"Another topic for another time," he said.

"Have a seat," I said and indicated the chair near the sofa.

Instead, he sat down right next to me. "Oh," I said and swallowed hard.

"I have information for you that might be interesting," he said and slid closer to me.

"Go on," was all I managed to say.

"Merrill's ex-wife was involved with a man named Jerry Sprigs. I assume you've heard of him?" he said and brushed a strand of my hair off my cheek and behind my ear.

"I have," I said. "He's kind of creepy."

"Well, Stella and Jerry have been having an affair for a long time. Since before Merrill and Stella got divorced. It's one of Coventry's worst-kept secrets. The only person who doesn't know is Jerry's delightful wife, but I suspect she knows something."

"That's probably why she's so hostile," I said more to myself than to Azriel.

"Anyway," he said and put his hand on my knee. "Word is that Merrill was going to tell Jerry's wife. He was attempting to extort money from Jerry, and Jerry couldn't have his wife finding out. She actually owns the majority of his business. It's the only reason he hasn't left her to be with Stella. Jerry was distraught over this, and I heard that Stella was willing to do anything to hold onto him. Perhaps, they killed Merrill together."

"If they were going to kill someone over that, then why not Jerry's wife?" I asked.

"Because Jerry's wife has a will, and in that will, it stipulates that on her death, the majority of the business transfers to her brother. If she dies or divorces Jerry, he loses his business."

"Interesting," I said.

"Isn't it, though?" Azriel asked.

He leaned in closer to me and his hand slid halfway up my thigh. I felt the butterflies explode in my belly, and a shiver ran down my spine. Everything about him drew me in, but in my head, I knew I wanted him to back off. It was just getting my head to convince my heart and my body to listen.

My heart.

I saw Thorn's eyes and bow-shaped lips flash in my mind. I remembered how safe and cared for he made me feel, and it mostly broke the hold Azriel had on me.

"Well, thank you for the information," I said and stood up quickly.

Azriel stood up too and suddenly we were chest to chest. Well, he stood a head above me, but we were so close. His hand was on the small of my back, and he was drawing me in again. "We've only just begun, Kinsley," he whispered seductively.

Resist, I told myself.

"You should go," I said and put my hands on his chest.

Trying to push him back was like trying to move a solid block of ice. He was hard, cold, and immovable.

Well, he would have been for anyone but a witch. I felt a storm brewing inside of me, and Azriel must have seen it in my eyes. He took a step back.

"Don't be that way, Kinsley," he said, but that time his murmurings had little effect on me.

"I thank you for the information, but you should go. I don't feel like company anymore," I hissed.

"Don't be angry with me," he said with a smile. "Or do. It makes you even more beautiful."

Suddenly, Meri was at my feet and I felt even stronger. Azriel took another step back.

"I'll go, but we're not finished," he said.

"Even if you call in your favor, you're not going to get what I think you want," I said.

"Oh, Kinsley... I would never use my favor for that. For that... you'll be begging me."

With that, he turned and headed for the door. I locked it as soon as Azriel was outside, and then went to the window to watch him leave.

My heart sank because as he was getting in his black Escalade to leave, Thorn's cruiser pulled up to my house.

Azriel pulled out of the driveway, and I waited there for Thorn to get out of his car. He didn't, and eventually, he started the car again.

He was going to leave. I had a bad feeling, so I ran outside and across the lawn. Thorn shot me an angry look and started to pull away from the front of my house.

"Thorn, wait. Please!" I called out.

He stopped. He sat there for another few seconds, but eventually, he turned the cruiser off and got out.

"Thorn, please come inside," I pleaded softly.

He gave me a nod and followed me into the house. Once we were inside, he didn't move away from the front door.

"I should go," he finally said. "I shouldn't even be this angry. This is ridiculous. You can do what you want. It's not like you belong to me. We've been on one date. Of course you can see other people. I just didn't expect..."

"I'm not seeing anyone else," I said. "Please don't go. Come in and sit down."

"I'd rather stand for now," he said.

At least he wasn't leaving, I told myself.

"He did make a pass at me, but I turned him down and kicked him out," I said.

Thorn let out a deep breath, and I saw him visibly relax. "You still shouldn't have invited him into your home, Kinsley. You knew what he wanted. Please don't try to pretend you didn't. I know you're smarter than that."

"You're right, but he's gone. It's over now," I said. "I let him in because he said he had information for me."

"I told you I would take care of that," Thorn said.

"I know, but do you want to hear it?"

"Sure," he said and rubbed his stubble.

I told him everything Azriel had just relayed to me about Stella and Jerry. Thorn listened, but he just shook his head when I finished telling the story.

"It's an interesting theory, but I don't have any evidence right now to back it up. I'll look into it, though."

"Now will you come in?" I asked. "Please? We can watch a movie on my laptop or something. I have those split headphones."

"I'm still in my uniform," he said.

"I don't mind, and if you do, I'm sure I can dig up some sweats and a t-shirt somewhere in this house. It's kind of what it does," I said.

"Sure," Thorn said. "That would be great." He smiled mischievously and the sparkle returned to his eyes. "Hey, are you trying to lure me in for Netflix and chill?"

I laughed. "I'm only offering the Netflix, mister. I'm a lady, after all."

Chapter Nineteen

The next day, I went into the shop to do some dusting and other cleaning tasks. I didn't anticipate it would take long as I was reasonably sure I could use magic for that and it not be considered personal gain. I was wrong and immediately got a huge puff of dust in my face. I had a sneezing fit that left me gasping for breath, and I swear I almost peed my pants too. Meri never would have let me live that down, so I went out to my car and grabbed some rags from the trunk.

After dusting, I went to the store and got cleaning supplies for the shop. Since I wouldn't be able to use magic, I'd need a stock of the stuff for regular cleaning and disinfecting. I'd already brought sage and salt from home to do any spiritual disinfecting.

In fact, I was in the middle of smudging the place with white sage when Jerry came through the front door again. "I wasn't expecting to see you so soon," I blurted out and almost dropped the smudge stick.

"Are you getting high?" he asked. "I've never seen a joint like that before."

"It's not a joint, and no, I'm not getting high," I said. "This is a sage smudge stick. I'm cleansing the negative energy."

"So, it's like incense?" he asked.

"Yeah, it's like incense," I just decided to go with that.

"Well, if I'd have known you were burning that stuff, I wouldn't have come in now," he said.

'Then the sage is doing its job," I mumbled under my breath.

"What's that?" Jerry asked as he stepped away from the sage smoke.

"I just asked if you were here to finish the plumbing job," I said.

"Oh, yeah. I found the part I needed in some of my old stock. Stuff I never got around to throwing away, but hey, it paid off," he said. "Since I didn't need to order it, I figured I'd just drop by and finish. I hope that's okay."

"Sure, I know you've got a lot of other work to do, and you're doing this as a favor to Castor. I won't be in your way."

"So, this place is just for tourists?" Jerry asked as he walked toward the back. "Right?"

As much as I loathed to do it, I followed behind him. "Yes, it's because of all the witchy tourist stuff. The witch and ghost tours go right by here, so I'm going to capitalize on that," I said. "Why do you ask?"

"I'm not sure if I should say anything," Jerry said, and it almost sounded like he was afraid.

"You can say anything you want," I said. "I'm not going to judge you."

I worried for a moment that he'd take that as a sign to make a pass at me, but what he said next caught me off guard. "It's just that there's something kind of off about this place. I mean, it's really nice what you've done here with the herbs, candles, and crystals. It's real pretty and all, but there's just something kinda... spooky."

"Good," I said. "I think the tourists will like that."

"And the other day, when I was fixing the commode, I saw something," Jerry said, and I noticed he was a little paler than normal.

"What?"

"It was gone in less than a second, but when I stood up from fixing the commode, I swear I saw something in the mirror behind me. A woman. She didn't look alive at all. Her skin was very pale, and it was almost gray. I couldn't tell if her eyes were angry or sad. She was there and gone so fast. Gave me the willies, though," he said and shivered.

"I think this back room is a bit spooky," I said. "Not nearly enough light. I'll stay back here with you while you finish."

"That would be great," he said. "Not much freaks me out, but I'd never seen anything like that before."

One thing I knew for sure, I wasn't going to have to worry about Jerry coming around and bothering me at the shop. He looked like he was ready to leave and never come back. I'd have to remember to thank the ghost later.

When he was done, he shut the bathroom door and hurried back out to the front of the store. I briefly wondered if I should take the chance of being alone with him and ask him about his relationship with Stella. He was in an emotionally vulnerable state because of being scared of the ghost, so I figured it might be a good time to ask. Another part of me knew it was better if I let him leave as soon as possible. Ghost or not, he might start acting like a sleaze again.

I didn't get a chance to say anything though, because the door opened and Madeline came into the store. "I know you're not open, but I was hoping it would be okay if I stopped in and had a look," she said. "There's a buzz around town about your store, and I've even heard that some tourists are extending their stay so they can be here when it opens."

"Really?" I asked. "I wonder how that happened. I haven't done any advertising."

"Oh, it's Viv over at the Brew Station. She's really been hyping it up to the tourists who come into her shop for coffee."

"That's really sweet of her. I'll have to go over there and tell her thank you," I said.

"Anyway, my curiosity was getting the better of me. I stop into the Brew Station every morning for coffee, and she's been talking about it for the last two days. I know it's probably rude for me to just drop in, so I'm sorry," Madeline said.

"No, it's fine," I said. "Jerry was just finishing up some plumbing work, but you can take a look around if you'd like."

"Thanks," Madeline said. "I think I'll take you up on that."

"Well, I'm going to go." Jerry said, and I tried not to let my relief show too much.

"Thanks for coming in and fixing the problem so fast. I do appreciate the work."

"Just have Castor call me if you need anything, or you can call me directly. I can bill him for you."

As soon as he was gone, Madeline made her way back up to the front. "I did want to see the store," she said. "But I also wanted to ask you if you found out anything more about why Merrill was coming in to see me that day. It's been bothering me."

"I haven't found out anything yet. I guess the sheriff hasn't been able to tell you anything either?" I asked.

"No. It doesn't help that I have nothing to go on. I just heard that you might have been making some headway in the case. I was hoping you might know something."

"I don't, but if I do find out something, I'll come to you first," I said.

"Thank you," Madeline said. "I appreciate it. The store is great too. I'll come back when you're open."

We said our goodbyes and I locked up the shop since I was done with the cleaning. On my way out, I ran into Thorn.

"Looks like I got here right on time," he said.

"Well, if you hadn't, I'm just going to get a latte and go home," I said. "I'm not too hard to find."

"Let me buy you that latte, then," he offered.

"I'm not going to turn down free coffee," I said with a smile.

We went over to the Brew Station, and Thorn ordered my hazelnut latte and a large dark roast for himself. I thanked Viv profusely for spreading the word about my new store. We probably would have chatted longer, but the lunch rush was starting for her.

Thorn and I didn't want to take up a table since we weren't eating, so we headed back out to our cars. "I'm not going to be able to stay long anyway," he said. "I wish I could, but I've got more information on the case. I have to see if I can run down any leads because of it."

"Is that why you came?" I asked. "Are you going to share the information you got?"

"I am," he said and stepped closer to me. "But this is between us. I trust you, and I don't want this going anywhere. Give me at least a fighting chance to do my job, Kinsley."

"I will. I promise I'll keep it to myself."

"Okay, so the medical examiner finally did an autopsy. What she found out was that Merrill was actually shot. She said it looked like the knife wound was there to cover the bullet wound. It was like they wanted to throw us off."

"And it worked," I said. "But wait, if that's the case, then it was someone who knows about that stuff. Also, the murder couldn't have taken place at the diner. The customers inside would have heard the shot. Unless they used a silencer?"

"I think it's more likely that the diner was a dump site. It was set up to look like that was where the murder took place, but it was actually committed somewhere else," Thorn said. "That's what I have to start trying to figure out."

"I understand," I said.

"If you understand, then you know you have to stay out of this. A killer is dangerous enough, but this person knew what they were doing. They're smart.'"

"And I'm not?" I asked.

"You know what I'm saying. Stay out of it, please. I promise I'll call you later."

He kissed me quickly on the lips and then went around to get into his cruiser before I could say another word. "Thanks for the coffee," I called out as he shut his door.

I got a wave back from him from inside the car, but after that, Thorn pulled out of his parking spot and left. I figured I'd at least try to do what he asked and stay out of it, so I headed home.

Chapter Twenty

At home, I was climbing up the walls wondering how I was ever going to stay out of the investigation. The new information was eating away at me, so I just kept pacing around my living room. Meri watched me with annoyance and interest from his perch on the edge of the coffee table.

"What are you doing?" he finally asked. "You're making me nervous, and that's almost impossible to do."

"I need to figure out where the primary crime scene is located. That's the key to this whole thing. I just know it, but how do I find it?"

"I don't know... I mean... You're a witch and all. Have you considered scrying for the location?" he snarked.

"That's it!" I said and jumped about two feet in the air.

Meri jumped too and scrambled back a bit. "You need to calm down," he said as his little tail flicked back and forth across the table. "Seriously."

"No, what I need is a bowl of water, some black food coloring, and a crystal pendant."

"I don't know where you will come up with all of that," he said sarcastically.

"Hush. You're messing with my vibes, and I need to be on point for this," I said.

"Yeah, because we all know what happens when you're not."

I just harrumphed at him and went into the kitchen to fill a bowl with water. There was black food coloring in the pantry, and I didn't know if that's because it's something witches always keep on hand or if the house supported my scrying efforts. Either way, after I grabbed a quartz on a silver chain from my stash of amulets, I was ready to scry.

I put the bowl on the kitchen table and lit some white candles around it. Meri jumped up on the table and sat nearby my setup while I took a seat in the closest chair and made myself comfortable.

"Okay," I said. "I'm going to get started."

Meri reached out with his little paw and touched the bowl once. He then proceeded to climb off the table into my lap where he curled up into a little ball.

I held the crystal over the bowl and let it swing around a few times. After I lowered it and started a ripple across the surface of the black water, I set the pendant off to the side.

My gaze was directed at the surface of the water. I watched it intently as the ripples began to slow down and clear. When they stopped was when I would see a vision, if I was going to get one at all. I had to stay laser focused or I could miss whatever message came through the water mirror.

"Something's happening," I said, and Meri jumped back up on the table so he could look too.

I did not get the vision I was hoping for. Instead, my heart began to pound nearly out of my chest as I saw a woman's hands pull a gun out and shoot me dead.

Chapter Twenty-One

The only clue the scrying provided, other than that it was definitely a woman who killed me, was that her nails were painted black with burgundy tips. I thought the nail polish looked familiar, but for the life of me, I couldn't remember from where. I'd seen so many women since I'd arrived in Coventry, and I couldn't remember what their hands looked like.

Just in case my memory of the nails was a false one and I hadn't actually seen them before, I decided to talk to someone who I hadn't yet. I'd spoken with Katy Shoals' brother, but I hadn't talked directly to her. Perhaps she'd gotten tired of Merrill's abuse and had taken matters into her own hands.

Her brother, Kevin, told me she worked as a groomer at Paws and Claws. "We're going to go get your nails trimmed," I said to Meri.

"What?"

"Just go with it. I need to talk to Katy Shoals at Paws and Claws. You're the only pet I have."

"I'm not a pet, and I'm not going," he said.

"She's really good. Her brother told me," I said.

"And I'm just supposed to believe him?" Meri scoffed.

"Come on, Meri. You eat demons for breakfast. You can handle a little nail trim. Don't be a baby."

"That's not funny," he said.

"I didn't mean it literally," I said and had to stifle a chuckle.

"I'm glad we've crossed over to the point where my... current state is amusing to you," he said.

"Aw, come on. It must feel pretty good to be so young again. Don't you have tons of energy?" I asked.

"Even if I did, I wouldn't give you the satisfaction of admitting it."

"Fine," I said. "But I need to talk to Katy Shoals. So, are you going to help me or not?"

"Fine. Whatever," he said. "I'm not riding in your purse, though."

"Deal."

We drove over to Paws and Claws and parked in the small lot next to the building. I'd never been inside before and was surprised to find it very much resembled a human hair salon. Instead of salon chairs, there were tables, but it was all very swanky. You could see the groomers working on dogs, but there was a reception desk just inside the door with a small waiting area.

"Hello. Welcome to Paws and Claws, how can I help you?" a petite woman with jet black hair asked me from behind the desk.

"I wanted to get my kitten's nails clipped," I said. "I've heard such good things about Katy Shoals, and I was hoping she was available."

I held up Meri so the woman could see him. He mostly fit in one hand.

"Oh my gawd. Aw!!!" she cooed and reached out for him. "I'm Katy Shoals. I'd be more than happy to take care of the little guy. You have excellent timing, I'm between appointments."

"Thank you," I responded.

"Would you like to come back with me or wait here in the front?" she asked. "You're welcome to do either."

"I'll come back with you. He's such a tiny baby, I'd hate for him to be away from his mommy," I said and watched as Meri glared at me.

"Oh, I totally understand. Well, right this way. I'll have you in and out in a jiffy."

I took Meri back to one of the tables and put him down. Katy grabbed a set of tiny pink clippers and started snipping his nails. I was about to bring up her relationship with Merrill when I noticed her fingernails. They were pink and sparkly. While it was possible she changed the color in the last couple of days, I ruled that out when I realized she was wearing acrylics and there was growth near her cuticles. She'd had her nails done that way for at least ten days and possibly two weeks. Katy wasn't the person I'd seen in my vision, so I didn't believe she'd killed him. But, I still wanted to know why she'd dyed her hair black.

"Your hair color is beautiful," I said. "Did you get that done at a local salon?"

"I did," she said. "But I'm thinking of getting rid of it. I only did it because my boyfriend said that darker hair would make me look less washed out. He said the blonde made me look sick."

"That's not a very nice thing for him to say."

"I'm starting to realize that, but he's gone now. It doesn't matter anymore."

"I'm sorry," I said. "I hope you'll be okay."

"I think I will be," she said and handed Meri back to me. "I would never wish for anyone to die, but now that he's gone, I've gotten a lot of perspective on how bad things were. Now I have another chance at life."

After that, we walked up to the reception area, and I paid for the nail trim. I left her a tip too because she really had done an excellent job. Even when we got out to the car, Meri said it wasn't as bad as he'd thought.

As we were leaving, I couldn't help but wonder what had led a beautiful girl like Katy to get involved with a loser like Merrill Killian.

Chapter Twenty-Two

I was rapidly approaching a dead end in the investigation. Katy hadn't been the woman I'd seen in my vision, and after talking to her, I felt it in my heart she wasn't the killer. She was better off with Merrill dead, but she hadn't murdered him.

My last hope unless something new came up was Stella and Jerry's affair. I did not want to talk to Jerry again, so I drove to Mann's Grocery Store. I thought that maybe if I confronted Stella about the affair, she'd confess. It was a long shot, but I was rapidly running out of ideas.

Stella was at the customer service desk, and when she saw me come into the store, she immediately came out from behind the counter.

"Outside," she said as she breezed past me.

I turned and followed her out to the area where we'd talked before. She pulled a cigarette out of her pack and lit it with a unicorn lighter.

"This whole town knows you're looking into my ex-husband's murder. I can't be seen talking to you at my work," she said and took a deep drag.

"I don't want to bother you," I said. "But I know that you and Jerry are in a relationship. I also know that it started before you and Merrill got divorced."

"So?" she asked.

"So, Merrill was threatening to go to Jerry's wife. Your boyfriend would have lost everything."

She let out a huge sigh and took another puff of her cigarette. "Yeah, but I was with Jerry the night Merrill died. We were at Totally Tanked all night," she said. "From right after I got off work at five until we got kicked out after one."

"Totally Tanked," I said.

"Yeah, it's the old tavern out by the mill. I know you've heard of it before. It's been in Coventry for at least twenty years," Stella said.

"And neither of you left at any time?" I said feeling myself deflate.

"Nope. No need to. We got burgers there for dinner and there are plenty of drinks, darts, and pool. All the entertainment we needed."

"What does Jerry tell his wife when he's out with you half the night?" I asked.

"Heck if I know. That's not my business," Stella said and took another drag. "I assume he tells her he's working on a job late and then says he got in right after she went to sleep."

"Well, thanks," I said.

"I'm actually sorry I can't help you more," Stella said. "You seem like a real nice woman. I hope you find what you're looking for."

After that, I left. I sat in my car for a few minutes and debated whether I should go check her alibi at Totally Tanked. On one hand, I figure I was going to find out she was telling the truth anyway. On the other, I knew I'd always wonder if I didn't at least go ask.

I found Totally Tanked on Google and got the address and directions. In a few minutes, I was pulling into their nearly empty parking lot.

The inside was about what you'd expect. It was a dark wood bar with dark tables and booths with green seat cushions. There were two pool tables and several dartboards.

I made my way up to the bar where there were already two older men nursing beers. I couldn't be sure if they'd arrived recently or they'd been there all day.

"Can I help you?" a bartender asked from the opposite end of the bar.

I walked down to where he was standing so the other bar patrons couldn't hear our conversation.

"I'll take a Coke please," I said.

He eyed me suspiciously. "Is that all?"

I pulled out a ten-dollar bill and slid it across the bar. "Keep the change."

"Sure thing," he said and grabbed a glass for my soda.

He made my soda from syrup and the carbonated water dispenser behind the bar. I'd never seen one made like that before, but I guessed that was how they used to do it.

The bartender placed the soda in front of me with a paper wrapped straw and pocketed the ten-dollar bill I'd given him. It was only after watching him do that I realized that sodas were probably free.

I drank about half my soda before the bartender came back down and stood in front of me. During that time, he'd been getting the other two men a new beer.

"So, why are you really here?" he asked as I took another sip of my fountain soda. "I do a decent job mixing up a Coke, but I know that's not why you came in."

I bit my bottom lip and thought it over for a moment. I'd come in to ask him a question, I figured I might as well ask it. "Were you working the night Merrill Killian died?"

"I was. I work just about every night. It's my bar, and I practically live here. Why?"

"Do you know Stella and Jerry?"

"Very well. They are two of my best customers," he said.

"Were they in here the night Merrill died? Like the whole night without leaving?" I asked.

"They were. From just after five until I kicked them out at closing," he said, and I felt my heart drop. "You know, the sheriff has already been in here and asked me the exact same thing."

"Well, thanks," I said and finished off my Coke in a couple of big gulps. "The soda really is good. Better than what you get at restaurants and stuff."

"Come back anytime," he said. "Even if you don't have questions. But I'll let you in on a little secret, the sodas are free."

"Hey, why can't I get free drinks?" the man at the very end of the bar groused. "I'm as pretty as she is."

"Shut up and drink your beer, Richard," the bartender commanded.

The man at the end of the bar started grumbling something about going to a nicer place with better service, but I couldn't catch it all.

"You're not going anywhere," the bartender said. "You've been banned from every other establishment that serves beer in this county. So, shut up and drink your beer."

The man, Richard, grumbled some more, but he did go back to drinking his beer and watching the television hanging over the bar. There was some sort of poker tournament going on, and it caught his attention quickly.

"Thank you again," I said and pushed the empty glass across the bar to him as I stood up from my stool.

He gave me a nod, and I left.

Chapter Twenty-Three

When I left the bar, I was feeling completely defeated, but I was also hungry. Usually, the best cure for that combination was a huge, greasy bacon cheeseburger and fries. I wanted to drop in and see how Reggie was doing too, so I headed for the diner.

There weren't many cars in the parking lot since it was after the lunch rush but before most normal people had dinner. I pulled into a spot near the door and made my way inside.

The sign that said "please seat yourself" was near the door, so I found a booth close to a window. I didn't see Reggie, and eventually, another waitress came to my table. Her nametag said Ginger, and she looked annoyed. As soon as she saw me looking at her, she replaced her scowl with a smile, but I'd already seen her.

"Where is Reggie?" I asked as she approached my table. "I was hoping to see her."

"Reggie didn't show up," Ginger said and smacked a wad of pink bubble gum. "I was supposed to have the night off. My sister is ticked because I had to drop my kid off at her house at the last minute. She didn't even call. Reggie has never just no-called, no-showed a shift."

"I wonder if something happened to her grandmother," I said and pulled out the phone.

"Naw, I already thought of that. I called over to Shady Acres. They haven't seen her either."

"I should go," I said, feeling suddenly panicked.

I didn't know if it was my intuition telling me that something was very wrong or the appearance of my uncle's ghost out in the parking lot that spooked me. He was closer than he usually got, but fortunately, he was on the opposite side of the building from my car.

As I was crossing the parking lot, a memory struck me like lightning. I remembered where I'd seen those black and burgundy nails. Suddenly, some things started to make sense.

I had to put some distance between myself and Brody's ghost, so I drove away from the diner and to the edge of town. Once I was fairly certain he was gone, I used my phone to find the location I was sure was the primary crime scene and also might have been where the killer had taken Reggie.

"But why would she take Reggie?" Thorn asked after he picked up the phone, and I explained everything.

"She was sniffing around earlier. I wonder if she's gotten desperate," I said.

"Kinsley, please calm down," he said, and I felt myself bristle. I hated being told to calm down. "You don't even know if Reggie really missing?"

"She is, Thorn. She didn't show up to work. She didn't call. She's not with her grandmother."

"She could be with her grandmother now. Maybe she wasn't there yet, or maybe Shady Acres made a mistake."

"Fine, call them yourself. Call me right back," I said and hung up before he could argue with me more.

I told myself that if he didn't call back in five minutes, I was going. Something was very wrong, and if I couldn't make Thorn believe me, then I was going to go save Reggie myself.

"She's not there." Thorn said when I picked up.

"I'm going," I said. "You can believe me or not, but..."

"Let's just check her house here first, okay?" Thorn said. "I mean, maybe that place is the crime scene, but perhaps she didn't go that far with Reggie. It will only take a few minutes to check her house and Reggie's, okay? Please, Kinsley. That cabin is outside of my jurisdiction anyway."

"Fine, what's her address in Coventry?" I asked.

He gave it to me. "And don't you dare go inside without me," Thorn said. "Please."

"I will wait for you," I said. "But I'm more worried about you than I am me."

Chapter Twenty-Four

Thorn got to the house two minutes after me. I know that because I was counting the seconds. He pulled into the driveway and blocked in a massive black SUV.

"Her car is here," Thorn said as I hurried over to him.

"She could have another one. Lots of people have more than one," I said.

"I'm going in to check it out. You stay out here," he said.

"You've got to be kidding," I said.

"No," Thorn said firmly. "I'm not kidding. This is an official investigation. I know you figured this all out, but you're a civilian. Let me do my job."

"Official investigation or not, you got this information from my vision," I said.

"We'll work that out later. Right now, I want to go see if Reggie is in there. If she is, then I need to go save her."

"Fine," I said. "Go, please."

The house was a massive, red brick structure with a white carport area supported by Greek columns on the side. Thorn didn't go to the front door, but instead, he ran around to the side door under the carport.

He pounded on the door a few times, but unsurprisingly, no one ever answered. I was actually a little shocked when he reared back and kicked the door in. Maybe he'd heard something inside that worried him, though.

That thought had my stomach in knots. I tried to stay outside, I really did. As I was about to step inside the house, a little black streak came barreling in my direction.

Meri ran into the house before me. "You didn't think you were going to go in without me, did you?" he asked as I followed him in.

He sort of skittered across the linoleum in the mudroom, but Meri managed to get control of himself. "You all right?" I asked.

"I'm fine."

Just then, we heard a muffled sound from the other room. I rushed toward it and nearly tripped over Thorn. He was laid out on the floor with a nasty knot forming on the back of his head.

I knelt down and put my hand gently on the back of his head. As I was healing him, Madeline appeared before me. She had her gun, the same one I'd seen in my vision, pointed at me.

"Get up," she said.

Thorn began to stir, so she pointed the gun at him.

I stood up and put myself between the two of them. "Lower your gun," I said.

"Or what?" she said and laughed.

"Fine, we'll do it your way," I said and waved my hand in front of her.

She dropped the gun, and I quickly stooped to pick it up. Her face was horrified as I aimed it at her. I could tell she had no idea why she'd dropped the gun when I waved my hand, but the magic in the town kept her from putting the pieces together.

"While Sheriff Wilson gets himself together, I think you should tell me why you're doing this," I said. "Also, back up. Is Reggie in there?"

I backed Madeline through her kitchen and a small pantry area. When we emerged in her dining room, I found Reggie tied to a chair. I made my way over to her and untied her with one hand while keeping the gun pointed at Madeline. She was unhurt but seemed pretty ticked off.

"This chick kidnapped me!" she exclaimed as she jumped out of the chair. "How did you find me?"

"We'll worry about that later. Thorn should be okay any minute now, and he's going to arrest her," I said. "So, Madeline, why'd you do it?"

"I know you think it's because I was having an affair with him," she began. "But you'd be wrong. That was one time, but I kept him on the hook with promises of more. I just wanted information, and Merrill wasn't very bright. He kept feeding me information thinking that if he made me happy, I'd sleep with him again. Ugh. I was really drunk the one time it happened."

"But that doesn't explain why you killed him," I said. "Why, if he was giving you information?"

"Because he stumbled on a bribery deal that I was... involved with. It was just easier to get rid of him at that point. I couldn't have him poking around in it more. So, I lured him up to my family cabin with the promise of a fun night, and I took him out. I've been involved with the law for so long that I thought I could cover my tracks forensically. So many people hated him that I never thought they'd figure out who did it. That was until you started poking around. I was so close..." Madeline said. "You ruined everything."

"Put your hands behind your back," Thorn said as he strode into the room with his gun drawn. "And, Kinsley, I've got this. Please place that gun on the table facing away from everyone."

One of Thorn's deputies took Madeline to the jail and booked her. Another gave Reggie a ride home and made sure she was safe. I offered to let her come over to my house so she wouldn't be alone, but she said she was going home.

"I'll call you if I change my mind," she said.

"You can. I'll come get you."

As she was leaving, I could have sworn I saw the deputy giving her a ride kiss her. It happened in a split second, though, and it was a topic for another time. I had to wonder if that's why she wanted to go home. *If it was, good for her,* I thought.

"Do you regret leaving me outside yet?" I asked Thorn as he approached me. "I had to save you, after all."

"You know I was just trying to protect you," he said and took my hand.

"And do your job. I get it," I responded.

"Do you?"

"I do. I'm not upset with you if you're not upset with me," I said.

"Why would I be upset with you?" Thorn asked. "I mean, you did save me."

"I did."

"You have to stay out of sheriff's business, though," Thorn said as he pushed a strand of hair off my cheek.

"I will."

"Will you?" he asked skeptically.

"I'll try."

"I guess that's the best I can hope for," Thorn said with a laugh.

And then he kissed me.

Epilogue

I wasn't able to avoid the welcome home party forever. Three days after Madeline was taken into custody, all of the Aunties showed up at my house. Everyone brought a covered dish except Lilith. She brought a keg and seven cases of wine.

The party lasted for hours, and there were even a few attempts to turn Meri back into an adult cat. They all failed. My spell was too powerful, but I hadn't figured out how to break it either.

They had to stop trying when my neighbors started showing up to see what was going on with the party. I didn't live that close to anyone, but the Aunties could get wild.

We invited everyone who showed up to the celebration, and pretty soon, I was sure half of Coventry was there.

I called Thorn to see if he wanted to drop by for a while. "Hey, so you might have heard we were having a huge party."

"I've gotten a couple of calls," he said with a laugh. "I was putting off coming over that way to shut it down."

"Hey, how about instead of shutting it down, you come join us?" I said.

"I don't know."

"Come on. I'm sure the people who called you are here now partying anyway. All of my neighbors are here. Emma Langley is three sheets to the wind on a bottle of chocolate wine Lilith handed her when she wouldn't stop complaining. Your shift has to be about over."

"Is there food?" he asked.

"Oh my gosh, Thorn, there is so much food. It's nuts."

"Made by the Aunties?"

"Yes," I said with a laugh. "My mother and father whipped up something too. But really, there's so much food and a keg too."

"Ha ha. Which one brought the keg?" Thorn asked.

"Guess."

"It was Lilith, right?"

"It was indeed. So, are you coming over or what?"

"Yes," he said. "I should be there inside an hour."

"Okay, well come find me when you get here," I said.

"Will do, boss."

"I like that." I said.

"I thought you would."

When I was off the phone with Thorn, I went looking for Meri. I hadn't seen him for a while. He wasn't downstairs or outside with everyone who had sparked up the grill. I thought that was strange. You'd have thought he'd be there waiting for someone to give him a steak or even a hot dog.

I found him upstairs in my bedroom. Meri was sitting on the dressing looking at himself in the mirror.

"Are you doing some sort of spell?" I asked as I walked into the room.

"No. Just trying to figure out if I still hate this or not," he said and turned around to look at me.

"So, what's the verdict?" I asked.

"It's whatever," he said and jumped down. "Let's go get some steak."

                Thank you for reading!!!

Grab the next book in the series: <u>Midnight Magic</u>

© Sara Bourgeois 2020

This story is a work of fiction. Any resemblance to persons alive or dead is a coincidence.

Printed in Great Britain
by Amazon